MONSTERS WITHIN

ZAKIR JAWED BHATTI

Copyright © 2025 by Zakir Jawed Bhatti

All rights reserved. No part of this publication may be reproduced, stored or transmitted in any form or by any means, photocopying, scanning, electronic, mechanical, recording, or otherwise without written permission from the publisher.

ISBN: 978-1-0691981-7-4

To my lovely Wife

Table of Contents

Chapter 1: The Black Envelope 5

Chapter 2: Shadows and Secrets 34

Chapter 3: Frozen to the Core 65

Chapter 4: One Lost, One Found 99

Chapter 5: The Black Letter Game 126

Chapter 6: Turning the Tables? 152

Chapter 7: The Anatomy of a Monster 175

Chapter 8: The Monster's Last Laugh 198

Chapter 1
The Black Envelope

The gates of Jasper High creaked closed, and the buses packed with students filed out one by one, disappearing down the snow-covered mountain path that led to the outside world. Behind them, Richard Bennett stood motionless, his sharp eyes scanning the empty campus.

This was his home for the next eight days.

Jasper High, a private boarding school nestled in the mountains, was a place that catered only to the brightest, most ambitious students, the top 2% of the nation.

The rigorous, year-round program pushed its students to their limits, with just one brief respite each year: eight days during winter.

Even during these rare days of freedom, Richard wasn't truly free. The glass walls of the school, the cameras placed at every corner—even inside the dorm rooms—meant that he was never really alone.

The school was a maze, an architectural wonder that took its inspiration from the Royal Ontario Museum. Some students called it a prison. Cell phones were banned inside; the only way to reach the outside world was through scheduled landline calls.

As the last bus rolled out of sight, Richard turned to face the looming, silent structure of the school.

Richard's life at Jasper had always been meticulous, a carefully crafted persona. A fastidious student, his hair was never out of place, his pencil always sharp. But despite his perfect exterior, something had been eating away at him for weeks.

Richard reached into his desk drawer and pulled out a black envelope, its edges creased from being hidden away. As he unfolded the letter, his expression darkened.

In a low, barely audible voice, his words reverberated in the silence, as if they were meant to linger in the room.

"You tainted me, made me pitiful.

You made me a monster in the corner.

You silenced me. You ridiculed my false hopes.

You took the only thing I had.

I held out my hand to you and let you go.

You deleted me from your eyes.

Finally, you overtook me.

After eight days, walk up the path by the black spruce tree.

Under the clock tower, you will see someone dead."

Richard's fingers trembled as he folded the letter carefully. The words were haunting, and the promise of something terrible hanging in the air left him with an unsettling sense of dread. His thoughts were interrupted by a sharp crackle from the school's PA system.

The announcement was brief: "All students staying behind for the break please report to the cafeteria."

Richard stood and left his room without a second glance at the letter. He wasn't the only one stayed at the school. As he made his way down the narrow corridors, he passed by several empty classrooms and locked doors.

The cafeteria was near the heart of the school, its glass walls offering a clear view of the empty grounds outside. He could already see the other students gathering around a long, barren table inside.

Eva Mendis was the first to arrive. She sat silently her face vacant as she fiddled with the hem of her sleeve. Richard didn't acknowledge her. They didn't speak.

Next, Frank Galler was setting the table timidly, he fumbled with the plates.

A little while later, Michael Lee, the most excited in the group, ran into the room with his camera. "Welcome to the exclusive club of stay-behinds!" he exclaimed cheerfully, filming every face with a grin.

Michael quickly turned the lens to Eva, calling her the "prettiest girl in Jasper High."

Michael moved on to the next person. "Gary Miller, the angel Gabriel of Jasper High!" he announced, waving the camera toward a lanky boy who had his ear buds in, his face impassive. Gary didn't even flinch as he was filmed.

"Steve Butler, the stoic enigma," Michael continued, turning the camera toward a tall, immaculately dressed boy whose detached look seemed to say, I'd rather be anywhere but here.

The last person to arrive was Jason Lee, the school's notorious bully. His smirk was all too familiar as he slinked into the cafeteria, making no effort to be charming.

Michael's demeanor shifted his excitement deflating as he reluctantly pointed his focus at Jason.

Then Michael pivoted toward Liam Dawson, the one teacher who had chosen to stay behind.

"You're the one staying? I thought it was the English teacher," Michael asked, his voice overly bright.

Liam, with unkempt hair and a tired look in his eyes, replied, "I don't have a family or a girlfriend, so the Principal asked me to stay. What a cruel world."

Liam poured wine for the students. "You'd better not tell anyone I served you alcohol," Liam warned.

Jason replied, "I promise, but I'm not taking this as a model for good behavior."

"It's my 35th birthday this week, that's why I'm celebrating with you," Liam said.

Gray responded, "Oh, but you look over 40."

"Shut up, anyway, you're stuck with me," Liam shot back. "Let's enjoy ourselves for the next 8 days. Cheers!'"

They all took a sip from their glasses.

Liam continued, "I'm being forced to stay here, but why didn't you kids go home?"

No one answered. After a few moments of uncomfortable silence, Jason tried to lighten the mood with a joke. "If I go home, my stepdad keeps looking at my butt. He walks in when I'm in the shower," he said.

But the joke didn't land. The other students avoided his gaze, especially Eva, who shot him a look of disgust.

In the moment of dead air, Liam asked, "Are you going to study?"

Michael replied, "Are you crazy? They say you get cursed if you study during winter vacation, especially on New Year's Eve."

Liam surprised. "Did you know that story too?"

Michael said, "Yes, I know."

Liam responds, "Do you know how that story began? Why you won't make it into university if you study on New Year's Eve? I heard it from the maintenance staff, the bald man in charge. Exactly 25 years ago, just before the new millennium, you weren't even born that year. Only one female student remained, all by herself in the huge school."

Michael interrupted, "What about the teacher who stayed?"

Liam said, "Teacher?"

Michael replied, "Yes?"

Liam answered, "If a student chose to stay, they were responsible for themselves—that was the rule. Because of that incident, if a student stays at school, a teacher must also remain now. The rules were changed. Listen to this story. Even on New Year's Eve, she studied until late at night. She got tired and went to the second-floor break room for coffee. She was humming to herself while the coffee brewed, but something felt strange. The hair on her neck stood up. So, she lowered her voice, but then the singing got louder from behind her, from the empty corridor. The singing gradually grew louder."

Liam started humming, "oooooo."

Everyone looked a little scared, Jason, the most scared by the story, was the first to jump out of his seat when the campus-wide alarm suddenly started ringing.

***

A bloody hand grips the school's front gate as Liam leads a group of students—Richard, Frank, and Michael—through the snow.

Liam's flashlight cut through the darkness, revealing a man bleeding from the head. Richard and Frank rushed to support him, gripping his arms as Liam guided them with the beam of his torch, leading the way toward the school clinic.

Michael, however, feeling suspicious, stays behind and eyes his surroundings warily.

***

Inside the school clinic, Liam tended to the bleeding man while Richard called 911.

"This is Jasper High. We have someone who's been in a car accident," Richard said into the phone. He looked at the injured man and added, "They want to know how bad it is."

The injured man responded, "I walked all the way here. I don't think anything's broken. I just hurt my forehead a little."

Richard spoke into the phone again, "He doesn't have any broken bones, but he hurt his forehead... Yes, he's fully conscious... Excuse me?"

Richard glanced at the injured man and asked, "Was anyone with you?"

The man answered, "No, I was alone."

Frank brought water to the injured man, who thanked him.

Once the call ended, Liam and Frank turned to Richard.

"What did they say?" Frank asked.

"They said that since the man's injuries aren't severe, they can't come right now because of the snowstorm. There's a huge highway pile-up, and they've got their hands full. They told me to call back if his condition worsens," Richard replied.

He then turned to the injured man. "Is there anyone you can call? Any family or friends?"

The injured man handed Richard a piece of paper with a woman's name, "Amanda," and a phone number. Richard tried to call, but no one picked up.

He called again. This time, someone answered.

"Is this Amanda speaking?" he asked.

She replied, "Yes."

Richard informed her, "Doctor John has been in an accident."

Amanda asked, "How is he?"

"He's okay, just minor injuries."

There was a pause. "Where is he now?" she asked, her voice tight.

Richard gave her the address of Jasper High, explaining what had happened as calmly as he could.

***

Meanwhile, in the cafeteria, Gary, Eva, Steve, and Jason were still eating dinner. Jason tried to lighten the mood, telling Eva, "You must be scared. There's a ghost in the girls' dorm... a humming ghost."

Steve grabbed his plate and, as he left, said, "Jasper High became a co-ed school in 2005."

Jason replied, "What?"

Steve smirked. "There were no girls in 1999."

Gary laughed, and Jason threw a tissue at him. Eva quietly left the cafeteria.

As Steve was about to enter his room, he bumped into Frank.

"What happened?" Steve asked.

Frank answered, "There was a car accident. Someone injured found his way to the school."

Outside the school, Michael stepped closer to the clock tower and began recording a video. Suddenly, a snowball hit his ear.

Michael turned around to see it was Jason. Michael adjusted his hearing aid and insisted, "It won't work if water gets inside."

Jason replied, "I know, it gets damaged because of water. I tested it before."

Michael said, "I remember—thanks to you, I couldn't hear properly for a week."

Jason apologized, "I'm sorry." He then grabbed Michael and started playfully scratching his head. "I'm sorry for everything. I apologize... forgive me."

Michael pushed Jason away and started walking off, but Jason followed.

"What do you want?" Michael asked.

"Forgive me, please? As you live life, sometimes things will upset you. I might joke around, but you could get hurt. All we need to do is say sorry and forgive each other," Jason said.

Then Jason pulled out the same black envelope Richard had shown earlier, waving it in Michael's face. "We can use words," Jason spat. "How dare you send this?"

As Michael bent down to pick up the letter, Jason shoved him to the ground.

Michael protested, "It's not me! I mean it."

Jason punched him, "Don't lie to me. Who else could it be? Who out of the other five? Richard? Steve? It has to be you! You're taking revenge because I messed with your hearing aid."

Michael pleaded, "Stop it... Jason, I didn't send you the letter!"

Jason punched him again. "Don't lie!"

Just as Jason was about to strike again, Richard and Frank stepped in.

Shaken, Michael pulled out a black envelope from his pocket. "I got one too," he said, his voice trembling.

Jason looked at him, stunned. "What? What's going on?"

Surprised, Frank admitted, "I got the same letter too." He turned to Richard and asked, "Did you get the letter as well?"

Richard nodded, "Yes."

Jason sneered, "What? It's just a spam letter then? Who dares to play such a sick joke like this?" He tried to open the school entrance door but failed. He pushed it hard, but it wouldn't open. Frank punched the keycard to unlock the door and said, "Liam said the safety level has been changed."

The four of them entered the school. Jason, still angry, stormed off to his room. Meanwhile, Michael was more concerned about his camera than his face. He cleaned it off and muttered, "I should have gone home!"

Richard turned to Michael and asked, "Do you think it's a joke?"

Michael replied, "Of course! I thought so from the beginning."

Richard asked, "Then why did you stay at school?"

Michael shrugged, "Well, because I'm a journalist, right?" He then walked off.

Richard turned to Frank and said, "Did you really think it's a joke, or did they make a fake letter to hide the truth?"

On the other side of the school, Liam was taking the injured man to the teacher's dorm. As they passed the security at the entrance, the injured man was impressed by how high-level it was. Liam explained, "It wasn't this extreme before, but there was an accident five years ago. A student broke into the teacher's dorm and set it on fire. That's when this security system was installed."

The injured man asked, "What happened to him?"

Liam responded, "Who?"

"The one who started the fire?" the injured man replied.

Liam sighed, "He jumped off the roof. He left a suicide note saying that his three years here were a nightmare."

The injured man looked amused and whispered, "A nightmare... so the kids here are inside someone's nightmare."

***

The morning light filtered through the narrow windows of the school hall as the seven students gathered. Each silently pulled out their identical black envelopes. The cold, glossy paper stared back at them like a symbol of the mystery that had suddenly consumed their winter break.

Steve was the only one who didn't pull out his letter. With a nonchalant shrug, he leaned back in his chair. "I threw mine away," he said casually.

Frank asked, "You did?"

"Yes. I didn't know what it meant," Steve replied.

The room fell silent for a long moment as the others exchanged uneasy glances. They all knew why they had stayed behind: the black envelope. The letter, with its cryptic and ominous message, had drawn them here. But Steve claimed he had stayed for "some quiet time to do some equation solving."

Jason, angry, muttered, "Some loser's playing a stupid joke."

Eva responded, "Really? Fine, if some loser is doing something stupid, let's tell Liam. He could help us figure out who sent these, even if he has to check the CCTV cameras."

But there was no immediate rush to agree. What if the danger was real? No one wanted to be the first to expose their vulnerability.

When Liam arrived in the hall a short time later, the students quickly shoved their black envelopes into their pockets. No one said a word. The question of the letters was pushed aside, hidden for the moment under a blanket of uncertainty.

Liam asked, "Why are all of you sitting here? Aren't you going to eat? Why aren't any of you answering?" Just then, the injured man also entered the hall. It was then that the group met the mysterious "Accident Man."

Liam introduced him as Dr. John Wilder, a psychologist who would be staying at the school until the roads cleared. He looked surprisingly fresh, having changed into a clean set of clothes since the night before. Gary wasted no time seizing the chance to get some psychological advice.

"I keep having this dream," Gary began.

Jason interrupted him with a joke, "I have a ringing sound that echoes in my ears."

Gary snapped back, "See an ENT doctor about that."

Then, turning to Dr. John, Gary continued, "A nude male ghost chases me around. Can you tell me what's wrong with me? Should I lie down on the sofa?" His voice was light and playful.

As Gary lay down on the sofa, the rest of the students huddled together. Dr. John asked, "Is this everyone?"

Liam replied, "Yes."

***

In another dorm, someone was watching the live stream from the school hall, captured by the security cameras.

***

Later, in the sunny afternoon, the mundane task of shoveling snow turned into a fun snowball fight for all the students. Only Richard broke away from the group, seeking out Dr. John for a private conversation.

Richard took a deep breath, enjoying the solitude, a brief escape from the noise and chaos of the others.

"Are you really a psychologist?" Richard asked.

"For now," Dr. John replied.

Richard hesitated before asking, "Can you tell a person's state of mind just by looking at the words they've written?"

Dr. John smiled faintly. "I can even tell their past... sorry, that was a lame joke."

Richard then said, "Someone I know wrote a kind of poem, and the contents are..." He trailed off, unsure how to proceed.

Dr. John, sensing his discomfort, answered, "The contents... other people shouldn't know about it, right? Priests and psychologists are both bound by confidentiality."

Richard nodded and handed Dr. John the black letter, unfolding it with care as if the paper might somehow bite him. "Can you analyze this? Do you think it's a joke?" Richard asked, his voice taking on a clinical tone.

Dr. John studied the letter for a moment, running a finger along the edges before looking up with a concerned expression. "Whoever wrote this is in a dangerous state of depression and aggression," he said gravely. "They need immediate treatment. But... there's more to it, isn't there?"

Frank, who had stopped playing in the snow to watch the conversation, lingered nearby, his eyes darting between the two.

Back inside the school, Frank found Richard in the hallway, and the two sat together in a quiet corner.

Frank asked, "What did the doctor say?"

Richard replied, "The doctor thinks it's not a joke."

While Gary quietly retreated to his room, he took an unmarked prescription, his actions deliberate yet discreet.

It was clear now that Richard had assumed the role of investigator, with Frank tagging along as his sidekick.

With focused intensity, Richard and Frank turned to Gary, pressing him about the letter.

"When did you get it?" Richard asked.

"Yesterday morning," Gary replied.

"Where was it?" Richard pressed further.

"In my locker," Gary answered.

Richard then asked, "Is the letter the reason you didn't go home?"

Gary, unfazed, glanced up and replied, "It's an honor. Someone hates me so much they want me to die."

Gary's usual apathetic facade shattered the moment Frank touched the statue of the Virgin Mary.

Gary's eyes snapped to Frank, and with sudden intensity, he ordered, "Put it down, immediately a little more towards the wall. If it's wrong, the Corner Monster could appear."

Richard's suspicion radar instantly pinged at the mention of the "monster in the corner." He recalled a line from the letter: "You made me a monster in the corner." His mind raced as he turned his attention back to Gary, who seemed disturbingly calm.

"Have you seen it?" Richard asked.

"Haven't you?" Gary replied.

"No," Richard said, his voice steady.

Gary asked, "Then why did you get the letter from the Corner Monster?"

Richard frowned. "What does it look like?"

Gary shrugged. "I don't know, I've never seen it properly."

"Then how do you know it's the Corner Monster?" Richard pressed.

"Because one side of its face is blue," Gary answered simply.

Gary's responses were simple, yet unsettling. He casually revealed that he believed the Monster in the corner had sent the letter, and that there was one in every house—at least, that's what his mother had told him.

"When did you see it?" Richard asked.

Gary's eyes darkened. "Since I was 5. After being kidnapped."

Richard's voice was steady. "Have you seen it in the dorms?"

Gary's gaze shifted to the Virgin Mary statue, he shook his head. "No, I have a lucky charm," he replied, his eyes lingering on the statue.

Richard couldn't help but wonder. "That blue part on its face... is it like a birthmark?" he asked.

Gary hesitated for a moment, said, "Perhaps."

***

Later, in the logbook room, Richard and Frank sifted through the record books, trying to find anyone with a blue birthmark.

As Frank flipped through the pages, his hand paused on Richard's own file. He saw that Richard's dream was to become a doctor and that he had listed his mother as his role model. But when Richard casually mentioned that his mother was dead, Frank faltered.

After a moment of silence, Frank asked, "Why is there no one with a blue birthmark? Did Gary lie?"

Richard sighed, his mind working through the possibilities. "Maybe it's because of hallucinations from his depression, perhaps."

***

Richard and Frank made their way to the school gym, where Steve was running on a treadmill, seeking any clues about a blue birthmark or the Monster in the corner. Richard asked, "Is there anyone with a blue mark in our school?"

Steve simply replied, "No."

Unable to resist, Frank quipped, "Steve probably doesn't even know what his classmates look like."

But to their surprise, Steve responded with unexpected insight. His voice was calm, almost detached, as he observed, "Out of the eight sins mentioned in the letter, 'You deleted me from your eyes'—that one fits me more than any of the others."

His disaffected attitude only deepened the mystery. Richard and Frank exchanged a glance. Richard then asked, "So, the letter is about different people?"

Steve nodded, his tone measured. "It could be either. One person committed all eight sins, or it could be separate people."

But it wasn't just Steve's indifference that bothered Richard. There was a deeper, more unsettling history between him and Eva.

So, Richard decided to visit the girls' dorm to meet Eva in the corridor. "It was after the fall festival in our first year... you were stalked for a while. Do you remember that? Someone sent you anonymous letters, and you thought someone was watching you all the time. You said you didn't like it..." Richard began.

He paused for a moment before continuing. "Then, you lost your USB and found a note in your locker that said, 'Look in the green sweater's pocket.' You rushed to the laundry room and found the USB in your green sweater. At first, you thought the stalker had taken it and then put it back in your pocket. But that wasn't true. You were the one who had forgotten it there."

Eva sighed. "When I think about what I did back then... I ran straight to you, scared. I asked you to protect me. Aren't I cute when I'm scared like that?" she said with a small laugh.

Richard reacted dryly, "You didn't act like that."

Eva shrugged a playful smile on her face. "I felt quite romantic, like I was the lead actress in a dilemma. And you were my prince."

Eva paused before teasing, "So, why are you digging into my past romance?"

Richard became serious. "After the USB incident, the letter you gave me without reading it. I just wondered what I should do with it. I published it in the school paper under my name. I thought the stalker would either attack me or just stop. After that, you didn't receive any more letters from the stalker."

Richard showed Eva the article he had published in the School newspaper. The title read JASPER HIGH SCHOOL. Eva began reading the poem aloud:

"To you, you are bad, you who shine even brighter without me... make my darkness so much thicker. Your name is bad, your name that I cannot say, it's bad because it's suit you so well. You are bad for laughing; my false hope becomes poison and makes me diseased."

Richard said, "If you didn't know it was from a stalker, it would just read like a love poem. Do you think it's a coincidence that the phrase about false hope appears in both letters?"

Eva paused, thinking for a moment, before replying. "So, are you saying I ridiculed his false hopes? And you're the one mentioned as someone who took the one thing I had?" She shrugged lightly, as if it didn't bother her. "Of course, someone wants to kill us. Someone's heart was used as a tool to aid in first love. I admit it."

As Eva left, Richard noticed through the glass corridor window that Michael was outside, discreetly taking their photos.

Later that afternoon, Richard convened an impromptu meeting with Michael, Frank, and Jason, hoping to piece together the mystery of the black letters.

"This doesn't make sense," Jason said, frowning. "Seven people received the letter, but it mentions eight sins."

Michael leaned back. "There is someone among us who has committed enough crimes for two or more people."

Jason's face darkened. "You piece of—" He lunged at Michael, but Richard stepped between them before he could land a blow.

"Enough," Richard said firmly. He turned toward the whiteboard, where the contents of the letter and the names of the seven students were written. "Let's figure out how we're all connected. I can already see one link."

Jason folded his arms. "Okay, go on."

Richard took a marker and began drawing lines between names. "If we start with me—I was linked to Eva. I was in Jason's class during our first year. Now, I'm in Gary's class."

He looked at Frank. "What about you?"

Frank hesitated. "I'm in the same class as Steve, but that's it."

Michael scoffed. "Think carefully. Didn't Jason ever steal from you or beat you up?"

Frank's expression shifted as a memory surfaced, "yeah once at the Fall Festival."

Jason narrowed his eyes. "What are you talking about?"

Frank exhaled sharply. "Our class was running a sandwich shop. You were about to leave without paying, and when I asked for the money, you slapped me."

Jason scoffed. "Whatever. It was nothing."

Michael smirked. "See? You talk about beating people like it's nothing."

Jason clenched his fists. "Hey—"

Richard cut in before the argument could escalate. "What happened between you two?"

Michael shrugged. "Ask Jason how many times he's hit me."

Jason shot him a glare. "The more you talk back. The more I hit you,"

Michael's jaw tightened. "And the more I'm punished, the harder I resist."

Richard turned back to Jason. "What about you?"

"No one, except Michael," Jason replied.

Michael cocked his head eyes locked on Jason and asked him. "What about Gary? I heard you could buy a building with the money you took from him."

Jason's temper flared, and he took a step toward Michael, fists clenched.

Richard grabbed his arm. "Tell me everything. We promised to keep it a secret."

Jason let out a bitter laugh. "You've got to be kidding me. You already decided I sent the letter. You're just trying to make me fit into your little puzzle. Is this a targeted investigation?"

His eyes locked onto Richard, burning with anger. "If you want to do it properly, start over with yourself. Why didn't you mention Steve? You try your best, but you can never beat a born genius like him. You're Salieri to his Mozart. You wish he wasn't around. You want to kill him, don't you?"

Jason's words struck a nerve, and before Richard could respond, he noticed Steve standing in the doorway, silently listening.

Then Steve spoke. "Aren't you guys going to have lunch?"

As everyone filed into the cafeteria, the atmosphere felt a little lighter.

Gary, however, remained hidden, lost in his own world up in the rafters. When he finally reappeared, Jason greeted him with a smirk.

"Hey, Angel Where were you?"

Gary responded with his usual cryptic detachment. "Angels are in heaven. Men are on Earth."

Dr. John, still adjusting to the strange dynamics of the group, looked up, puzzled. "Why is Gary's nickname 'Angel'?" he asked, genuinely curious.

Jason, with a slight chuckle, explained, "He's 'Angel' because he got here by donating a lot of money. Not because he has wings."

Gary didn't seem bothered by the teasing. As always, his cool demeanor hung around him like an invisible cloak.

Eva, unable to resist poking fun at Jason, pointed her spoon at him from across the table. "His nickname is 'Plague,' and I'm sure you can guess why."

Jason shot her an irritated glare.

"What are you looking at?" Eva taunted. "I thought we were sharing nicknames."

Before their verbal sparring could escalate, Michael suddenly interrupted his expression serious. "I heard something on the radio earlier," he said.

"There's a murderer still at large. No one knows why he did it. No one understands his motive."

Jason shrugged. "Sounds like just another crazy lunatic."

Michael frowned. "If he was crazy, wouldn't his neighbors have noticed?"

Jason's gaze grew colder. "Haven't you seen what the neighbors always say after a criminal is caught? 'He was always kind and quiet. Why would he do such a thing?'" His voice took on a mocking tone, mimicking the bewildered testimonies from news reports.

Eva shot back without hesitation. "If you ever got caught for something like that, this is what I'd say: 'Well, I knew this would happen one day.'"

Jason's expression darkened instantly. "If I did such a thing, you'd be the first victim."

The words remained, casting a heavy mood over the cafeteria. It was a line no one should have crossed—and yet, there it was.

Then, Steve, ever the philosopher, broke it. "Are monsters like him born that way, or are they made?" His voice was casual, almost academic, but the weight of the question settled on Dr. John like a stone.

Steve leaned back thoughtfully. "Murderers must have some kind of problem—maybe a genetic flaw, a malfunction in their DNA. If they were born that way, then it's not their fault. It's just a disability. So is it fair to punish them?"

The table fell into an awkward silence.

Steve continued, "But what if they weren't born that way? What if they were abused, hurt, or went through trauma that pushed them toward crime? Is it still their fault?"

Dr. John tilted his head, brow furrowing in thought. "So, you're saying that criminals shouldn't be punished."

Steve almost scoffed. "Of course they should be punished. Society can't function otherwise. I'm just wondering—if we don't understand why they are the way they are, is it fair to criticize them emotionally?"

Richard, who had been listening quietly, finally spoke. "It is right to criticize," he said firmly. "Even if someone has trauma, problems, or a bad upbringing, they still make a choice to commit a crime. They know it's wrong, and they choose to do it anyway. That's why they deserve to be judged."

***

Unbeknownst to them, their conversation was being watched. In a dimly lit dorm room, a young man with striking red hair sat hunched over a laptop, chewing gum and blasting loud rock music.

***

After the meal, Doctor John found Gary alone and approached him. He apologized for asking about the nickname earlier.

Later on, Gary, in his usual strange way, simply replied, "It's okay. It's my fault for being born into a rich family." He wasn't being sarcastic. He really meant it.

Up in his room, Gary stared blankly at the unmarked pills on his desk before reaching for a velvet-lined secret box. His hand trembled slightly as he took the pills.

Meanwhile, Eva visited Dr. John in the school's clinic, complaining of a headache. He handed her some medicine, but it wasn't the medication that caught her attention—it was the large, jagged scar on his palm.

"That's a huge scar," Eva remarked.

Dr. John glanced at his hand and smiled slightly. "A stalker cut me once. Sometimes, patients get obsessed with their doctors."

Eva frowned. "What happened to the stalker?"

Dr. John's smile didn't fade. "They're quiet now," he said, almost too casually. "But they still appear out of the blue sometimes."

In the school's computer lab, Richard and Frank were searching for any references to the "monster in the corner."

"There's no fairy tale or legend about monster in the corner or blue monsters," Frank said, scrolling through pages of information.

"Nothing overseas either," Richard added.

Frank sighed. "Maybe Gary's mom just made it up."

Richard's expression darkened. "If Gary sent the letters, it would make sense. He's unstable, and he has every reason to hate all of us."

"Why?" Frank asked.

"That nickname—'Angel.' He hates it, but we still call him that, both to his face and behind his back."

Before Frank could respond, a loud crash echoed from Gary's room. They rushed to the scene, only to find Gary smashing his Virgin Mary statues into pieces.

"It's all useless now," he muttered, his eyes wild. "It's here already."

Gary hallucinates that one of his many mirrors is reflecting something eerie—a small boy huddled in the corner of the room, half of his face disturbingly blue.

Meanwhile, in the school clinic, Dr. John observed Eva closely. "You're just like the others," he said. "Patients who come to see me often have something to say but don't know how to start."

Eva hesitated. "Then what do you do?"

Dr. John tapped his pen against the desk like a metronome. "I start talking about the weather. Or a film I watched. Or I might mention the car accident from the other day." He paused, his voice dropping slightly. "I almost died recently, you know."

He continued tapping the pen, humming a folk song. "I heard this song as my car was flying off a cliff," he mused.

On the other side of campus, in the boys' dorm, Richard stood over Gary's secret stash of drugs, his expression unreadable. He turned to him.

"What does the monster in the corner look like?"

Gary hesitated. "It's usually a child," he admitted. Richard's curiosity deepened. "A child? Are there any exceptions?"

Gary nodded slowly. "Only once."

"When?" Richard pressed.

Gary's voice was almost a whisper. "On campus. First year. I was sleeping alone when I heard a voice. When I opened my eyes, I saw a man… half of his face was blue."

"Do you remember anything else?" Richard asked.

Gary lay down on the floor, lost in thought. Frank looked at Richard. "What should we do? Should we tell Liam?"

Gary suddenly murmured to himself, "It's better to remember quickly… What did you do to the monster in the corner?"

Richard tensed. "What did you do, Gary?"

Gary blinked his expression distant. "Me?" His memories crashed into him like a tidal wave.

"That night, when I saw that man, I got scared and started screaming—'Monster in the corner!' That's how I gave him the name. And then… then it really became a monster in the corner."

His voice softened. "If I had called it a flower… it would have become a flower."

As Richard and Frank turned to leave, Gary suddenly muttered, "Eva… Eva…"

Richard spun back around. "What about Eva?"

Gary's eyes darkened. "The monster likes Eva."

Richard frowned. "What do you mean?"

Gary voice faded as he drifted into sleep. "Monster in the Corner dropped a wallet. It landed right in front of me... Inside, I saw a picture of Eva."

Back in the clinic, Dr. John kept tapping his pen, still humming that eerie folk song. Then, he said something unexpected.

"You know, when my accident happened, scenes from my past didn't flash before my eyes. But time... time slowed down. The world outside moved in slow motion. As if time was sagging. Everything was silent... except for that song. Do you understand?"

Eva's lips parted slightly, but she didn't respond right away. Soon, words escaped her—fragment of her past spilling out, memories slipping through her grasp.

Dr. John listened, singing softly as she spoke.

***

As Eva finally left the clinic, she felt strange—disoriented, as if an unseen force was guiding her steps. Before she knew it, she was standing at the base of the clock tower. The snow swirled thick around her, shrouding her from the world.

Meanwhile, Richard and Frank remained in the hallway, still lost in thought over Gary's words. Then, through the window, they saw Eva outside. Suddenly—she collapsed.

They ran toward her, their breaths quick and shallow, their faces frozen with fear as they neared the clock tower.

They found Eva lying still in the snow—her body pale against the white. A crimson stain spread beneath her wrist. She had cut herself.

Chapter 2

Shadows and Secrets

Eva lay motionless on the school clinic's bed, her face pale against the stark whiteness of the sheets. Dr. John stood nearby, his brow furrowed in concentration as he checked her vitals, his hands moving methodically.

In the teachers' dorm, Liam sat next to Richard, studying Eva's profile. After a moment, he began his questioning. "Tell me about Eva's personality."

Richard's jaw tightened as memories surged back. "Every society has ranks, and the same applies to school. There are a few ways to determine status here—Steve is known for his grades, Jason for his strength, and Eva for her looks. There were other beautiful girls, but only Eva's smile could make others feel warm. She was at the top of the school's social hierarchy. She was loved, and she enjoyed being loved. Suddenly she changed completely as if her personality had been rewritten. There was no trace of who she used to be."

Liam nodded. "When did you and Eva break up? I'm not talking about the school's rules—I want the truth. Did she change after your breakup?"

Richard's eyes flashed, his fists clenching at his sides. His voice came out low but sharp. "No. She changed first."

Liam's gaze didn't waver. "Why did she break up with you?"

Richard took a deep breath, his expression distant, as if retrieving something buried deep within. "I don't even know what happened."

Liam studied him carefully, sensing there was more to the story than Richard was admitting. But before he could press further, another thought surfaced—something that had been gnawing at the back of his mind.

Liam voice was calm but firm as he asked, "Are you hiding something? Last year, only two students remained at school. This year, there are seven. That's strange, don't you think?"

Meanwhile, in the school hallway, Michael showed Frank the pictures he had taken of Eva earlier. The images were stark—capturing her lifeless form, blood staining the snow where she had fallen.

Michael then handed his camera to Jason, who looked through the photos without flinching. After a moment, he passed the camera back.

Michael muttered, "Under the clock tower, you'll see someone dead—just like it was mentioned in the letter. Does that mean we'll be killed by an undefeated murderer? But how could one person possibly kill all of us?"

Jason scoffed. "You fool. Eva tried to kill herself."

Michael's face paled. "No, it sent a telepathic message to make Eva kill herself. Oh no... we're all dead now!"

Jason smirked slightly. "Let's say I suddenly wanted to die."

Michael muttered, "Please do."

Jason ignored him and continued, "What method would I use? I'd hang myself in my room or jump off the roof—quick and certain."

Michael whispered, "Hallelujah."

Jason went on, his voice serious now. "But on this freezing day, she walked all the way to the clock tower, trudging through snow up to her knees. Why? Why go there?"

Suddenly, Richard appeared.

Jason turned to Richard. "What did Liam say?"

Richard didn't answer. "Hey!" Jason called again.

But Richard stormed past them, his face twisted in frustration and rage. He didn't even glance at Michael, Frank, or Jason as he made his way straight to his room, his entire body tense, his steps heavy.

Jason and Michael exchanged a look before following. As they neared Richard's room, the unmistakable sound of his fists pounding against the door filled the hallway.

The sound was harsh, relentless—each strike shaking the door as if he were trying to break it down with his bare hands.

Jason and Michael flinched as the force of the blows vibrated through the air. Richard didn't stop. His knuckles were raw, bleeding, but he kept going, hammering the door with fury.

Liam sat in the school security center, his eyes locked on the small screens before him, the security footage rolling in real-time. He clicked pause, rewound, then zoomed in on a grainy image—Eva, trudging toward the clock tower.

The footage was eerie, but it didn't offer answers. Nothing explained why she'd walked so far through the deep snow, why she had chosen that place. His fingers hovered over the mouse as his mind raced with theories, but all he had were more questions.

Meanwhile, Richard had his own mission. He sat with Michael in the school's rest area.

"Do you still have the footage from last year's trip?" Richard asked.

Michael blinked. "Of course."

"Check if there's a man with a blue face," Richard said.

Michael frowned. "A blue face? You mean like Avatar?"

Richard shook his head. "It was during a school trip. The students dressed up for the talent show. Look for anyone wearing blue makeup or a mask."

Back in his room, Michael pulled off his hearing aid, letting silence engulf him. Plugging in the footage, he focused on the screen, playing each frame in rapid succession, scanning for anything—anything that might stand out.

Meanwhile, Frank was doing the same in the school's multimedia room, absorbed in his search. His concentration was broken by a familiar voice.

Liam leaned against the doorframe. "What are you looking at?"

"Footage from the school trip," Frank replied.

Liam exhaled through his nose. "I should've stayed outside. I'm good at singing and dancing." A trace of bitterness laced his voice.

Frank glanced at him. "Why didn't you?"

Liam shrugged. "I couldn't. Someone passed out. I had to bring him back to the hotel."

"Gary?" Frank asked.

"Yeah," Liam said simply. "Turn off the lights when you leave."

Frank nodded, turned back to the screen, his focus sharpening.

He was determined to find something—anything—that would finally make sense of all this.

At school clinic, Jason peered through the cracked door, watching Eva.

Dr. John caught him, his steps measured as he approached. "The scars are superficial," the doctor said. "She didn't bleed much. She'll be fine. You don't need to worry."

Jason smirked. "Why would I worry about her?"

Dr. John wasn't fooled. "This school is interesting," he said thoughtfully.

Jason scoffed. "Yeah, Jasper High, Prison High."

The doctor studied him. "What interest me most are you students. The faces you show to others… and the ones you wear when you think no one's watching."

Jason turned on his heel and fled, locking himself in his room. He threw the bolt into place and even barricaded the door. Slumping into his chair, he tried to steady his breathing. But before he could calm down, a hand gripped the back of his chair.

Jason's body stiffened his heart pounding in his throat as he slowly turned his head. Behind him stood a red-haired boy, casually chewing gum— the same boy who had been watching them through the CCTV cameras. He met Jason's gaze with a predatory grin.

"Hey, Plague," the boy sneered.

Jason's bravado dissolved. He scrambled to his feet, lunging for the door, but it was too late. The deep, mocking laugh of boy echoed through the room.

Meanwhile, Michael was still absorbed in the footage, oblivious to the chaos unfolding. With his hearing aid removed, the distant sound of Jason's desperate screams never reached him. Gary, Steve—all of them were isolated, locked in their own spaces, alone with their thoughts.

But Richard and Frank were in the hallway when they heard the commotion from Jason's room.

They rushed to the door. Richard shoved against it, but it was locked tight. Gritting his teeth, he rammed his shoulder into it. Just as he thought it was useless, Frank joined him. Together, they charged, and with a loud crack, the door splintered open.

What they saw stopped them cold.

A boy stood in the center of the room, a cruel smirk playing on his lips as he held Jason by the collar.

Jason's face was pale with terror. Frank's voice cracked. "Mad David?"

David's grin widened. He seemed to relish the fear emanating from Jason.

"Save me!" Jason pleaded.

David's focus shifted toward Richard and Frank. Seizing the moment, Jason bolted for the door, but David lunged, attempting to grab him again.

Richard stepped in, yanking David back with surprising force. "Enough! What are you doing here? You stayed at School without permission, and now you're using violence? If a teacher finds out, that's a week in the detention room."

David scoffed. "Thanks for worrying about me, but I'm already expelled. Do you think a dead man cares about punishment?"

He took a step toward Jason again. Richard intervened, "Wait—at least tell us why."

David smirked. "Ask Jason why."

Jason stammered. "I don't know! He's a psycho! He just attacked me out of nowhere!"

David's eyes gleamed with malice. "You think you'll get away with it?" he sneered. "I may live a hopeless life, but I don't stick my nose in other people's business. The statue... I didn't break it."

Richard's expression tightened. "Then who did?"

David pointed at Jason. "Me?" Jason shouted. "Why would I do that?"

David said "Fireworks were stolen from the storeroom—two boxes. What did you do? Throw a fireworks festival?"

Jason shook his head furiously. "You think I took them? No way! Who told you that?"

David shrugged. "I don't care. I've decided it's you." He took another step toward Jason, who shrank back.

Richard cut in. "David, If you didn't blow up the statue, your expulsion can still be reversed. If we find the real culprit, you might be off the hook."

David snorted. "Richard, step aside. I'll find the truth my way."

Richard stood firm. "But no one can know you're here or that you used violence... Aside from the statue incident, you'll exceed the penalty limit. Your expulsion hasn't been officially decided yet. I'll speak to the principal once vacation is over."

David rolled his eyes. "Pointless. Liam will know by now anyway."

Richard turned to Jason. "You won't talk, right?"

Jason nodded quickly, terrified.

David smirked. "What makes you so sure?"

Richard took David to his room and showed him the black letter.

David's eyes flicked over it. "So, you all got this letter. And no one told a teacher? Interesting that means... you're not as innocent as you look."

Later, Richard and Frank met outside Jason's room.

"What did he say?" Frank asked.

Richard sighed. "Jason insists it wasn't him. I think even if he stole the fireworks, he couldn't have done it alone. The bomb had a manual timer. Jason isn't capable of that."

Frank frowned. "What about David?"

Richard shook his head. "David was scouted."

Frank's brows shot up. "What?"

"David got a three-year scholarship. He was in the top percentile of middle school students."

Frank was stunned, "Really?"

Richard nodded. "He even outshone Steve in their first year. Didn't you know?'

"No," Frank admitted.

Richard's voice was firm. "I don't think David has anything to do with the statue or the letter."

***

The next morning, Richard was jolted awake by a sudden, forceful shove. Disoriented, he blinked up to find David standing over him, a wicked grin plastered across his face. "What is it?" Richard muttered his voice groggy. "It's still early."

David scoffed. "How can you sleep, Richard?" His voice dripped with mockery. "Think a little deeper about the one who sent you that letter. You should be trembling at the curse between the lines—show some respect to the writer. Who do you think sent it?"

Richard rubbed his eyes and sighed. "I don't know."

David's was enjoying this—the unease creeping into Richard's face. "You don't even have a theory?" David shook his head in disappointment.

Richard's temper flared. "Same goes for you too," he shot back. "Someone hates you enough to steal fireworks, build a bomb, and time it perfectly to go off when you stepped outside—right in front of the statue. And you don't know who did that either, do you?"

For a moment, David's expression flickered, a crack in his usual confidence. But it was gone as quickly as it came, replaced by his signature Cheshire grin.

"You only start fights and curse at people when you dislike them," David mused, his tone disturbingly calm, "If you really hate someone, you don't make it obvious… real hatred? That's done in secret."

His gaze drifted toward the window. Richard followed it, spotting Steve walking alone through the snow.

Richard tore his eyes away, his mind spinning with another question. "Is it really okay for you to just walk around like this, even with all those cameras?" he asked. "How do you come and go without getting caught?"

David shrugged like it was the most natural thing in the world. "I have my ways. It's easy when you know how."

Later, as Richard walked through the ground floor on his way to the school's clinic, he stopped in front of the locked security center. He stared at the door, a nagging thought forming in the back of his mind.

"Students aren't allowed in there," Liam's voice snapped him out of his thoughts.

Richard turned as Liam approached. "Good morning."

Liam eyed him. "What is it?"

Richard hesitated, asked, "If there was someone else at school—besides the nine of us—would you know?"

"There's no one else here," Liam said with certainty.

"Are you sure?"

Liam frowned. "Why? Do you think someone is here?"

Richard quickly shook his head. "No."

Liam explained, "Do you even know how many cameras this school has? More than hundred cameras including the dorms, every room has one. I was shocked at first, but what do you expect from a place where kids study eighteen hours a day? If studying was considered labor, this school would've been sued already. Are you still worried?"

Richard forced a small smile. "No."

But in reality, his mind was racing. How was David managing to move around undetected?

Maybe it was because of the vacation—no one was actively monitoring the CCTV. Even Liam rarely checked the footage.

And that thought left Richard even more unsettled.

Later, Richard found himself in the school clinic, tending to Eva. She lay motionless on the bed, her skin pale and lifeless, and dried blood still staining her hand.

Richard gently wiped it away, his fingers trembling slightly as he rolled up her sleeve.

The sight of the numerous scars lining her arms hit him like a punch to the gut. Eva stirred, slowly regaining consciousness. She blinked, noticed Richard's actions, and winced. "It hurts," she muttered before immediately yanking her sleeve down, hiding the scars from view.

Richard couldn't bring himself to look away. His voice was quiet, almost hesitant. "Why? What is this? You... Why did you do this?"

Eva's reply came quickly, flat and deadpan. "Because of you," she said her voice empty. "After I broke up with you, I couldn't stand it. Are you happy now?"

Richard knew better. The words didn't ring true. Deep down, he understood that Eva wasn't revealing the full story. She wasn't just blaming him—there was more, something deeper.

Eva's eyes darkened and she leaned back against the pillow, a sad, bitter smile curling at the corner of her lips. "It has nothing to do with you... whether I stab myself or whatever! Just be polite and pretend you don't know."

Richard's voice was strained. "How can I pretend not to know you?"

Eva scoffed. "Then you should've acknowledged our relationship and me a long time ago when I was really lost. I understand you were burdened by a girlfriend who suddenly changed. You were concerned it was against the rules, and exams were coming up. I heard your dad found out about us too. When I said I wanted to break up, I bet you were relieved. It was too late then," she murmured. "But now, it's really too late. So don't worry about me."

Richard felt something twist in his chest. "Fine, I am not your family, and I am no longer your boyfriend, but I can't ignore you. There's something strange about you," he muttered.

"Yes, I am strange, but I'm not the only one," Eva replied quickly.

"Look at Gary, Jason, and Michael. They're all abnormal too. If you want to help someone, look at them. No, better yet—look in the mirror. You feel so guilty—that's abnormal too. If you slit your wrist, everyone would understand. 'The child who lived in place of his mother—he killed himself.' That's what people would say."

Eva's words were like daggers to him. Richard flinched, unable to respond.

His pent-up frustration boiled over as his fingers clenched around a pencil, snapping it in half with a loud crack.

At that moment, Steve barged into the room, his presence immediate and unwelcome.

"Don't whine either, then. You keep whining and telling him not to notice you. It's your life—do whatever you want, but don't burden others," Steve snapped at Eva.

"If you want to die so badly, do it quietly when no one's around."

Richard intervened. "Steve—"

Eva reacted just as sharply. "Steve— Fine! I won't die at school! Happy?" she shot back, her voice void of emotion.

Richard turned to leave. Steve was already gone, off to another confrontation.

But it wasn't long before Richard was swept into another matter. Michael showed the footage he had discovered— Jason during the school trip, holding a blue water balloon.

"This is from the second day of the school trip, from the hotel we were staying at," Michael explained. "I'm sure there was a warning not to throw them at people, but its Jason—the Plague."

At that exact moment, Jason entered the room and asked, "Where is Angel?"

Richard replied, "We don't know."

Michael joked, "You've sinned so much and you won't be able to see him."

Jason scowled. "You want me to hit you every day?"

Richard changed the subject. "What about Gary? I haven't seen him around. We don't want him to have slit his wrists too."

Then Richard showed the footage they were watching— the one where Jason was holding the blue water balloon. "Do you remember who you threw it at?"

Of course, Jason had no recollection of what had happened. "What's this about?"

Richard quoted from the mysterious letter.

"'You tainted me, made me pitiful.' So you threw a blue water balloon at someone's face, and he ended up in Gary's room, where Gary tricked him into thinking he was a monster in the corner. If you remember who you hit, we'll have our answer."

Jason scoffed. "You jerk keep trying to link me to that letter. And what's this 'monster in the corner' nonsense? Does having paint on someone make them a monster? It was just watercolor paint! Even if Angel is a little strange, how could he confuse that?" Jason turned and left in frustration.

Later, Jason crept through the dorm, trying to remain unnoticed. He slipped into Gary's room and returned a watch to the drawer, its initials—G.S.—gleaming under the faint light.

Shortly after, David, hidden and watching through the CCTV, waited until Jason was gone. He then entered Gary's room, retrieved the watch, and studied it with a calculating grin.

Still searching for Gary, Jason wandered into the school auditorium. Frustrated, he muttered to himself, "Where has he gone?"

As if the day couldn't get worse, Jason suddenly found himself face-to-face with David.

David asked "Who?"

Jason's panic soared as he was grabbed into a headlock. David forced him to listen as he pulled out the same watch that had belonged to Gary.

"I thought you'd go running," David sneered. "Why are you looking for Angel? Come on… tell me—what's the connection between you, Angel, and this watch?" His eyes glinted with curiosity.

Meanwhile, in the waiting area, Richard and Frank sat together. Richard read the black letter aloud: "'you tainted me, made me pitiful, you made me a monster in the corner.'

This part happened during the school trip last August. 'Eva ridiculed his hope, and I stole something of his.' That part took place in October."

Frank frowned. "Chronological order?"

Richard nodded. "Yes. Anyway, if we can figure out who Jason threw the balloon at, we'll have our answer."

Suddenly, Jason burst into the waiting area, panting heavily. "Come! Mad David will kill him!"

***

Outside the school, the evening sky was painted in shades of orange and purple, the sun dipping lower in the distance. Gary sat alone, enjoying the cool air, unaware of the storm about to crash down on him.

Without warning, David turned on him, grabbing him by the collar and delivering a few vicious blows. "Was it you?" he demanded, his voice a venomous hiss.

The confrontation might have escalated further if Richard hadn't intervened, forcefully pulling David away.

"Let go!" David snarled, but Richard held firm.

Gary, shaken but silent, hurried toward the school entrance. David tried to follow, but Richard tightened his grip. When it became too much to hold him back, Richard threw a punch—hard enough to make David stumble.

David wiped the blood from his lip and grinned. "You want to fight?" he taunted, eyes gleaming with dangerous amusement.

From a nearby window, Liam and Dr. John watched the scene unfold. The moment David spotted them he pulled his hood low over his face, masking his features.

Liam's voice was cool, almost amused. "What are you doing? Who's fighting who? Should I be the referee?"

Richard straightened, breathing heavily. "It's nothing."

Liam's gaze lingered before he shrugged. "It better be. Is it over now?"

Richard nodded. "Yes."

Satisfied, Liam turned away, walking with Dr. John.

The doctor glanced at him. "Is it really okay to leave them like that?"

Liam smirked. "Their blood's hot at eighteen. They need to cool off somehow."

Dr. John shook his head. "Still, I wasn't expecting that. It caught me off guard."

Liam chuckled. "I used to play sports. I'm a little generous when it comes to fights. It's not like they're ganging up on one guy—it's just between them. Better to let them sort it out themselves. Besides, Richard is there. He'll handle it."

***

Inside Richard's room, David sat at the head of the space, his eyes flicking nervously between the gathered students— Gary, Frank, Jason, and Richard.

"I have something to say before I begin the investigation," David announced, his voice steady. Then, turning to Gary, he asked, "Angel, you will tell the truth, whether it's to your disadvantage or not?"

Gary remained silent.

David scoffed. "You chose right to remain silent, huh? Then let me ask you— is it true that Jason stole the fireworks and sold them to you?"

Before Gary could respond, Jason cut in. "Gary, you gave me a watch!"

David shot Jason a sharp glare. "Shut up." Then, returning to Gary, he demanded, "What did you do with the fireworks?"

Finally, Gary broke his silence. "I gathered the black powder," he admitted, his tone flat, unapologetic. "And with that, the statue went bang! It wasn't explosive, so it wasn't that effective, as you all know."

Richard's brows furrowed. "Why?"

Gary leaned back and exhaled sharply. "Isn't it obvious? To put David into a trap."

David's eyes widened. "What did I ever do to you?"

Gary's lips curled into a bitter smile. "You ruined everything, David. My efforts, my determination, my future… the only chance I had to get out of this Alcatraz."

David looked genuinely confused. He raised a hand in objection. "Are you sure you've got the right guy?"

Gary let out a dry, humorless laugh and locked eyes with David. "Do you remember what you did during the Fall Festival?"

David scowled then smirked as the memory surfaced. "Oh yeah… I was planning an event to go down in school history! The bungee jump!"

Gary's face darkened. "That's right," he said through gritted teeth. "I had just started my performance. The auditorium had a hundred chairs, but people still had to stand in the back. I convinced the principal to build a band rehearsal room. I convinced Jason and the others to perform with me, even though they had to sacrifice study time. Do you think that was easy?! I put everything on the line. But because of your stupid stunt, the seats emptied before I even finished my first song."

David scoffed. "That's what this is about?"

Gary's hands clenched into fists. "Because of your crazy act, everything I worked for went down the drain! You wanted all the attention? I let you have it. Are you satisfied now? Now your name will go down in school history—as the first expelled student of Jasper High."

David shrugged. "My dynamic and popular act— I'm sorry it ruined your show, but all this over just one performance…?"

"A little performance?" Gary cut in, his voice seething with emotion. "My parents came that day. They told me they'd decide after hearing my song. If I impressed them, they'd finally let me leave this place—this hell, where all of you call me angel." His voice cracked, but he kept going. "And then you ruined everything."

David's smirk faded.

Gary's eyes welled with tears. He let out a broken laugh, shaking his head. "A little performance? A little performance?" His voice rose to a shout. "A LITTLE PERFORMANCE?!" Then, unable to hold it in any longer, he buried his face in his hands, sobbing.

Meanwhile, Michael sat quietly in his room, playing footage from the Fall Festival on his laptop. The video showed David standing on the school roof, preparing to bungee jump. The crowd below was electric with excitement.

Dr. John appeared at Michael's open doorway. On the screen, David made the jump, landing safely to a roaring cheer from the students. Even teachers were seen rushing toward him—among them, Gary's parents.

Michael looked up at Dr. John. "That was the moment he got the nickname Mad David. That's when his legend began."

Dr. John asked, "Did you know he was going to jump?"

Michael leered, "Of course. I was the cameraman. I set up three cameras. It was a huge project."

Dr. John sulked. "And it never occurred to you to stop him? It was dangerous."

Michael nodded. "David wouldn't have listened to me anyway. I just watch. It'd be cheating if I interfered."

Dr. John grinned. "Interesting."

Back in Richard's Room, Gary's head was buried in his hands.

David's stomach twisted. He hadn't realized how much pressure Gary had been under. After a moment, he exhaled and said quietly, "I'm sorry. Maybe it's too late, but… I'm sorry."

Without waiting for a response, David left the room.

Jason let out a breath. "That was… stifling."

Richard turned to Gary. "What will you do now? If we just let this go, he'll be recorded as a dropout."

Gary's expression was blank. "Whatever." Then, without another word, he walked out.

Richard, Frank, and Jason exchanged uneasy glances.

Jason, who had been silent for most of the discussion, shifted uncomfortably. "Maybe we should leave out the fireworks part," he muttered. "Gary never told me he was going to blow up the statue. If I'd known, I wouldn't have sold them to him. I'm not that brave. Let's just say Gary got the fireworks from someone else. If Angel's accused, no matter what, he'll be excused… but I'll be in serious trouble."

Jason hesitated, added, "And there's something else… I think Gary sent the black letter."

Richard looked troubled. "Why do you think that?"

"It's obvious. Gary wants to leave this place, but there's no way out. So he planned to destroy the school's reputation instead. Look at the people who got the letter—Steve, Eva, Michael, you, and me. He knew that if we all raised an issue with the principal, it might finally force them to let him go."

Frank scowled. "Then why did I get a letter? I'm nothing special."

"That was probably a mistake. It was meant for someone else," Jason replied.

Richard thought for a moment. "And what about the content of the letter?"

Jason waved dismissively. "He just wrote whatever."

Richard shook his head. "No, Jason. I know Eva's stalker was real. It wasn't Gary."

Richard arrived at the school clinic and found Doctor John seated in a chair, concerned about Eva's knife marks.

"Where is Eva?" he asked.

Doctor John answered. "She went out just now. Don't worry; she's much stronger than you think."

Richard glared. "She's just being stubborn."

Doctor John leaned back in his chair. "If she's being stubborn or even angry, at least she's displaying emotion."

Richard hesitated before asking, "Did you see her wrist?"

"You mean the knife marks?" Doctor John asked.

Richard nodded.

Doctor John sighed. "Yes, those marks bother me too. They imply that she cuts herself—not necessarily to end her life, but to feel something, to remind herself she's alive. Self-harm is different from suicide… But her sudden attempt at taking her own life—it wasn't natural."

Later, Richard found Eva in the cafeteria, eating as if nothing had happened.

Eva noticed him staring. "Is it strange, seeing me eat when I wanted to kill myself yesterday?"

Richard sat down beside her. "Tell me about yesterday."

"Why do you want to know?" Eva replied, her voice neutral.

"Why did you suddenly want to die? And why there—under the clock tower?" Richard pressed. "If you don't want to talk to me, I'll call someone else."

He stood up, about to leave, when Eva finally spoke.

"I don't know… It was like it wasn't me," she murmured. "Like I was in a dream or something."

Richard turned back. "Like you were on drugs?"

Eva thought for a moment. "A little... like I was floating in the air. I don't know. It was my first time. I've never fainted like that before."

Richard's eyes widened at her words. Something wasn't right.

Without another word, Richard rushed to Gary's room, a sinking feeling settling in his chest.

Gary's pillbox was open, and there was only one pill left. Richard's heart sank. He suspected Gary had given Eva one of the pills.

"Where's the other pill? There were two," Richard demanded.

Gary, high and disoriented, pointed to his tongue. "It's still there…"

In a fit of frustration, Richard flushed the remaining pill down the toilet. Gary looked at him, "Geez! That's cost a lot," he muttered.

***

Meanwhile, Jason was trying to convince Frank that Gary is the one who send the black letter.

"Motive is the first step in a crime," Jason said. "Gary has the perfect motive."

Frank, however, wasn't convinced. "But Doctor John told Richard that a crazy guy wrote the letter."

Jason leaned in. "Who's the craziest one in the school? Mad David or Angel? It has to be Angel."

Jason continued, "Gary lied about seeing the monster in the corner during the school trip. But you're not sure about that, are you?"

Frank said. "You threw the balloon with paint, too."

Jason's expression grew more insistent. "I threw the balloon with blue paint. It was just water paint; you can wash it off with water. How can Gary confuse that with a birthmark? I know Angel is weird, but that's not possible. It's impossible, you got that?"

At that moment, Richard stepped in. "It's possible if Gary was on drugs at the time. You can go check it out; he's totally blitzed."

Steve had been quietly listening to the conversation from the side.

Eager to test Richard's theory, Jason decided to visit Gary's room. He painted half of his face blue, stood in front of Gary. When Gary saw him, his eyes went wide, and he began to hyperventilate.

Still under the influence of the drugs, Gary saw Jason as the Monster in the corner. His hallucinations worsened, and he began seeing a child with half of a blue face sitting in the corner.

Jason, in a low voice, asked, "Do you know who I am?"

Gary sweats in fear. "Why? Why are there two of you?"

Jason repeated the question. "Do you know who I am?"

"Monster…" Gary whimpered.

Jason, relishing his role as the dark figure, grinned and said, "Tell me, I'll eat you up…" He didn't stop there. Jason started tormenting Gary further, enjoying the fear he was eliciting. "I am the monster in the corner, boo!"

Gary's fear skyrocketed as he began shaking and crying. He looked around frantically and then asked, "Why are there two monsters in the corner?"

Gary screamed, "Mom! Mom" His voice was full of desperation as he grabbed a guitar and began swinging it wildly through the air.

Richard, hearing Gary's screams, burst into the room just in time to see Gary collapse.

Gary cried out for his mom and aunt, a frightened child lost in his terror.

Richard quickly rushed to Gary's side, holding him as he passed out. Jason, still standing there, stammered, "I was just playing a joke…"

Frank quickly helped Richard lift Gary, whose body was limp from the shock, and together they carried him to the school's clinic.

Doctor John guided them to an exam bed and quickly began setting Gary up with an IV to help stabilize him.

Meanwhile, Liam called Jason, Richard, and Frank into the staff room at the teacher's dorm. His expression was tense—he needed answers.

"What happened?" Liam questioned his voice sharp.

Jason shrugged. "Gary just passed out."

Liam asked. "Do you think I'm stupid, Jason?"

Before Jason could respond, Richard stepped forward. "Gary was on drugs," he admitted. Then, he reached into his pocket and pulled out the black letter, handing it to Liam. "This is the letter that we all received."

Liam's expressions grow dim as he unfolded the paper. "And why are you telling me this just now?" he asked coldly.

At the same time, in another part of the school, David was watching everything unfold from his laptop.

***

Later that night, when Richard returned to his room, he found David sitting casually on his bed, waiting for him.

"I told Liam about the letters," Richard said, shutting the door behind him. "I didn't tell him about you. But you will get caught."

David leaned back against the wall. "I'm leaving early in the morning."

Richard just shrugged. "Whatever."

David tilted his head. "What did Jason do for Angel to fall?"

Richard didn't respond.

David's voice sharpened. "Don't ignore me. I am David."

Richard finally looked at him. "Mad David is nothing now. After spending a few days with you, I see you differently."

David let out a low chuckle. "I am Mad David of Jasper High. How did I end up being ignored by you?"

Richard had grown closer to him over the past few days, and now David could no longer hide his secrets.

With a smirk, David grabbed Richard's laptop and turned it toward him. "Open it."

Richard leaned in as David pulled up the school's CCTV system.

"No way" Richard's eyes dilated. "The security cameras... Did you hack the school's security system?" You could get expelled for that.

David grinned. "So keep it a secret then."

***

That night, David snuck into the kitchen, stealing food from the refrigerator.

Then David made his escape through the air ducts, crawling from the student dorms to the teacher's dorm. When he peeked through the staff room window, he saw Liam speaking with the principal.

"No, I just wanted to check," Liam said. "Sorry to disturb you."

As the call end, Liam sat down and began looking through a student's profile.

Once Liam was gone, David decided to sneak in and take a look at the profile Liam had been checking. Just as he leaned over to read the file, Liam appeared from the shadows.

Before David could react, Liam threw him to the ground with a swift judo move.

***

When David woke up, he was in the detention room—a glorified prison cell. His head throbbed as he looked up and saw Liam watching him through the Plexiglas window.

David winced. "I think my arm is broken…"

Liam jibed at David. "Don't fake it. I taught you how to fall." His voice was firm. "And that was self-defense."

David groaned. "You slammed an eighteen-year-old to the ground."

Liam folded his arms. "Proper punishment will lead you on the right path. That's my principle."

David smirked bitterly. "You could've killed me."

Liam ignored that. "Why were you hiding?"

David sighed dramatically. "I wasn't hiding. I'm just… shy. More shy than I look."

They both exchanged small smiles.

Liam's tone turned serious again. "What were you doing in the staff room earlier?"

David shrugged. "I went in by accident. This school is like a maze!"

Liam turned to leave. David sat up quickly. "Where are you going? Don't leave me here."

Liam glanced over his shoulder. "Think it over. You'll find a better reason for your actions."

David's smirk faded. "Don't do this to me. It's illegal."

Liam simply said, "Think alone and find peace in your heart."

David frowned as he glanced up at the wall above him. The same words were carved into the stone: Think alone and find peace in your heart.

Liam walked away, leaving David to his thoughts.

***

At the staff room, Liam deleted the CCTV footage of his altercation with David, ensuring there was no evidence left behind. He then made his way to the gymnasium, his mind heavy with thoughts.

Once inside, he went straight to the punching bag, striking it with sharp, controlled punches—each hit harder than the last. His breathing was steady, but his frustration was evident. After several minutes, he stopped, sweat dripping down his face. He took a deep breath and sat down in a yoga pose, closing his eyes in an attempt to clear his mind.

Doctor John entered the gym and hesitated before speaking. "I was watching you," he said cautiously. "But I was too scared to talk to you."

Liam opened his eyes but didn't move. His voice was calm yet firm. "Each competition has a defining moment, the moment when the winner is determined."

Liam looked straight ahead, lost in thought. "Both fighters may have the same skill and strength. But those who win medals, those who go on to represent their country… they know when that decisive moment comes."

Doctor John listened in silence as Liam continued.

"I was always second in judo," Liam admitted. "But I think… now is my decisive moment."

Later that night, back in the teacher's dorm, Liam received another call from the principal.

"Yes, Principal," Liam answered, keeping his voice even. "Nothing's up. Yes, everything is all right."

After the call ended, he sat down and looked at the file once more. The name on the cover was Tom Harris.

Tom Harris

Born: April 9, 2002

Father's Name: Martin Harris

Mother's Name: Katherine Harris

Eldest of two sons

Middle School Graduation Results: 1st out of 750 students

High School Entrance Results: 10th out of 150 students

Allergic to strawberries

Dreams of becoming a doctor

Died: January 3, 2024

Liam exhaled slowly, staring at the last line.

Cause of Death: Suicide — he jumped from the school roof.

Liam leaned back in his chair, rubbing a hand over his face.

A student with a bright future, a student who had once dreamed of saving lives… but had taken his own instead.

Liam exhaled sharply and closed the file.

Chapter 3

Frozen to the Core

It was the fourth day of the break, and the snow and ice had reached dangerous levels, making it nearly impossible to walk outside without slipping. The cold was biting as Richard stood by the window, watching the scene outside.

Eva sat beside the statue, bundled in her coat, while Michael wandered around aimlessly—until his foot suddenly slipped on the ice. He hit the ground hard. Eva burst into laughter.

Michael, lying on his side, noticed Richard watching from the window and smiled. "Hey, take a look at my butt for me. I might have a new birthmark."

A few minutes later, Michael entered the building, shaking snow off his clothes. Richard stood by the entrance, waiting as they walked inside together.

"Why is it so slippery out there?" Michael grumbled. "The snow melted a little yesterday then froze over again, and now there's fresh snow on top. It's a nightmare." He dusted off his coat. "I'm agile, so I didn't get hurt—but Doctor John wasn't so lucky. He hurt his arm."

Richard stopped. "What? How bad is it?"

Michael shrugged. "He fell on the ice this morning. He said he can't even move his arm."

Without another word, Richard headed to the school clinic. When he arrived, Doctor John was examining his own arm, his face unreadable.

"Are you hurt?" Richard asked.

Doctor John sighed. "Yes. Looks like I'll need to put it in a sling."

Richard helped him secure the sling properly. "Shouldn't you go to the hospital?"

"If I wanted to, I'd have to call a helicopter," Doctor John replied dryly. "I don't think it's that serious."

Richard hesitated. "What about breakfast?"

"I'll eat later," the doctor said, waving him off.

Just as Richard was about to leave, he paused. "Have you seen Liam?"

Doctor John thought for a moment, shook his head. "No. Not since last night."

At the cafeteria, Jason, Steve, Gary, Michael, Eva and Frank were already gathered, chatting over their meals. But Liam was nowhere to be seen.

"Where's Liam?" Richard asked.

"He hasn't come yet," Frank replied.

"May be he is still in bed?" Richard said.

Michael sneered. "Maybe he slipped outside and can't move."

Gary, chewing his food slowly, muttered, "Or maybe the monster in the corner ate him."

Jason leaned toward Richard. "You think he found something out?"

Eva shot Jason a look. "Are you worried?"

"Not as much as you," Jason countered with a smirk.

Meanwhile, Gary suddenly started eating at an alarming speed, shoveling food into his mouth.

Jason arched a brow. "What's with him?" He sighed. "Geez, how many days left until school starts again?"

Gary barely looked up. "Will we even be alive by then?"

Jason rolled his eyes and turned to Angel. "Hey! I don't believe in hitting people during meals. Cooperate with me." He then beamed at Gary. "You were on the floor crying last night, shouting for your mom. Help me, Mama!"

Gary froze. His grip on his spoon tightened.

Jason sneered. "Mama's boy."

Gary's chair scraped against the floor as he shot up. Before anyone could react, he grabbed his bowl and hurled it at Jason. The next second, he lunged across the table, tackling Jason to the ground.

"You bastard" Gary roared.

Chaos erupted. Richard and Frank rushed forward, Frank grabbing Gary and pulling him back before he could do more damage. Richard held Jason firmly in place.

"Let me go!" Jason yelled, struggling against Richard's grip. "That psycho hit me, and you just stood there!"

Richard turned to Gary. "What the hell is wrong with you?"

"He lied!" Gary shouted back, breathing hard.

Jason wiped his face, his fury barely contained. "Do you even know what happened last night?"

Gary's expression shifted. Confusion flickered across his face. "I—" His voice faltered.

Jason narrowed his eyes. "Do you even know who I am right now?"

Gary hesitated, said, "Jason, the Plague."

Then, without another word, Gary turned and stormed off.

Jason exhaled sharply. "He's crazy. His mind keeps coming and going! He should've been expelled a long time ago." He turned to Richard. "He's on drugs right now, isn't he?"

Before Richard could respond, Steve cut in. "Richard is he?"

Richard shook his head. "No. I flushed the last of his pills yesterday. And Right now… it's different. This isn't like when he was on drugs."

Steve looked at Richard intently. "Can you tell the difference? Between when Gary's on drugs and when he's not?"

Richard didn't hesitate. "Yes."

Steve leaned forward, voice low. "Then other people must have noticed, too."

Richard tensed. "Others? who?"

"The teachers," Steve said simply. "You said Gary had an incident after taking drugs during the school trip, right?"

Richard nodded slowly.

"Liam must have seen it," Steve added.

Later, Richard and Frank searched the campus for Liam, but he was nowhere to be found. They decided to check the teachers' dormitory. While Frank scoured the area, Richard knocked on the entrance door of the staff room. No answer.

Frank returned after a while, shaking his head. "He's not there."

Richard wondered. "Where could Liam have gone?"

Frank pondered. "Is our school really that big? I haven't seen David around either."

Richard hesitated before explaining, "David told me he was going home early this morning."

Frank looked skeptical. "I don't think so."

"What?"

"I didn't see any footprints in the snow outside. That means both Liam and David are still on campus."

***

Meanwhile, David was still locked up in the detainment room, desperately trying to break free. He jammed a pen into the door's lock, but it wasn't working. Frustrated, he began flailing his arms in front of the security camera, hoping someone would see him.

Luckily for him, Richard had gone to his room and turned on David's laptop.

Frank peered over Richard's shoulder. "What's this?"

"It's the school's live security feed," Richard explained, his voice low. "David hacked the system."

Frank's eyes widened. "Are you serious? That's dangerous."

"I found out yesterday," Richard admitted. He adjusted the settings. "If you put it on auto, it cycles through the locations where there's movement."

As Richard flipped through the feeds, something caught his eye.

"There he is," Richard said, pointing at the screen.

Frank leaned in. "Where is that?"

Without wasting another second, they rushed down to the detainment area.

David's face lit up as soon as he saw them. "Richard! Frank! I am so happy to see you."

Richard asked. "Why are you here?"

David scowled. "How should I know? Liam knocked me out as soon as he saw me and threw me in here."

"Liam?" Richard repeated.

"Yes!" David turned slightly, lifting his shirt to reveal a dark bruise on his back. "If that had been anyone else, they'd already be dead. My heart nearly exploded. How can this kind of human rights violation happen in a country like Canada?"

Richard ignored the dramatics. "Tell us the truth. What really happened last night?"

David huffed. "Ask Liam yourself. But first—open this door."

"We've been looking for him," Richard said.

David responded, "Maybe he went outside."

"In this snow?" Richard shot back.

David answered. "He's dumb and strong."

Frank cut in. "There are no footprints outside."

David's confident expression wavered for a second before he scoffed. "Look, I swear I didn't do anything. But I can tell you this—Liam was up to something. Don't you want to know what it was?"

Richard hesitated, but he stood firm. "Liam must've had a reason to lock you up."

Without another word, he turned and walked away, leaving David in the cell. Frank sighed and followed Richard down the dimly lit hallway..

"Hey! You can't just leave me here!" David called after them. "Richard! Buddy! Frank! At least leave me some food! I only had a piece of cream bread since last night…"

Richard and Frank headed back to David's room to check the security footage from the previous night. If David was telling the truth about Liam, there should be evidence.

But when Richard brought up the recordings, the footage from the night before was gone. Completely erased.

Frank questioned. "Did David lie?"

Richard stared at the blank screen. "I don't see anything from last night. It's strange. The teacher left the staff room at 11 PM, but after that… nothing. It's like Liam disappeared—or someone erased the footage."

A knock on the door interrupted their thoughts.

Richard and Frank stepped out of David's room, only to find Steve standing outside Richard's room, which was right next to David's.

"Richard," Steve said. "I need to talk to you."

Richard nodded. "I need to talk to you too."

As they walked toward the detainment area, Richard, Frank, and Steve discussed the strange events happening at the school.

Jason, lurking nearby, listened in.

Richard turned to Steve. "David is still at school. I think something's happened."

Steve's expression darkened, "really?"

Meanwhile, poor David remained locked in his cell, glaring through the plexiglass window as Richard, Frank, and Steve stood outside, staring at him.

Without a word, they walked away.

"…Seriously?" David grumbled. "You're just gonna look at me and leave?"

David slammed his fist against the door. "How can you leave me here?"

Moments later, Jason arrived at detainment area. He took one look at David locked inside and—without a word—turned right back around.

David groaned. "Unbelievable."

Steve, Richard, and Frank were walking down the corridor. Richard glanced at Steve and said, "Liam locked David in the detention room and then disappeared. Just before that, I told Liam about the letter."

The three of them made their way to the storage room, where Steve began searching for something. Richard asked, "What do you want to tell me?"

Steve pulled out a student pamphlet with Liam's profile and handed it to Richard. "Here," he said. "I saw this last time. Look at the teacher section, specifically the employment qualifications."

Richard flipped through the pages of the pamphlet while Steve continued, "Our school pays a high salary, but the standards are also high. You need at least five years of experience. You must speak a foreign language, and most teachers have a Ph.D. But Liam, the P.E. teacher, doesn't meet any of these criteria."

Richard replied, "Maybe because he played sports?"

Steve shook his head. "Art and music teachers' positions are temporary, but P.E. teachers are permanent. Since the second half of last year—right after the school trip—Liam became a permanent employee. Do you know who recommended him? "Mr. Miller the biggest donor to the school and the president of the school board of directors."

"Gary's father?" puzzled Richard asked,

"Yeah," Steve replied. "Now, how do you think this story goes? The P.E. teacher knew Gary had taken drugs on the trip."

Frank interrupted. "I heard Liam was the one who came back to the hotel with Gary when he passed out during the trip."

"We need to find Liam," Steve said, his tone serious.

Richard sighed. "We've looked everywhere. The only place left is inside the teacher's dorm."

Steve proposed breaking into the teacher's dorm to get answers. Richard hesitated. "That's off-limits. If we get caught, we'll be in serious trouble."

Steve didn't seem concerned. "I'll go alone if you don't want to join me," he said, unfazed.

Meanwhile, Dr. John sat in school clinic, popping painkillers for his injured arm. He watched as Steve, Frank, and Richard passed by his door, plotting their next move.

The three of them reached the teacher's dorm entrance. Richard asked, "Is it possible to unlock the door?"

"In theory, yes," Steve replied. "If 30,000 volts of electricity flow through the door, it becomes faulty. You should step back."

Without hesitation, Steve used a Taser to break the electronic lock. After a moment of uncertainty, Richard followed him inside. They began searching for Liam's room.

"Where's Liam's room?" Frank asked.

Steve opened a door, revealing a picture of Liam hanging on the wall. "Here," he said. "This is it."

Richard and Frank entered the room while Steve opened a drawer. He pulled out a black letter.

"That's the one I gave to Liam yesterday," Richard said, his voice a mix of confusion and concern.

At that moment, Jason appeared in the doorway, holding a book. He opened it to reveal another letter addressed to Liam. "Liam received a letter, too," Jason said.

Steve didn't seem surprised. "I think the part about 'silencing me' in the letter refers to Liam. He kept quiet about what he knew. When Richard talked to Liam about Gary and the letter, Liam remembered who was with Gary that night and who the 'monster' is. He called someone to confirm it, and David saw it. That's when Liam locked David up."

Steve's lips curled into a smile.

Frustrated, Richard snapped, "What are you smiling about?"

"It's amusing," Steve replied.

"You find this situation amusing?" Richard asked incredulously.

"Don't you?" Steve responded with a sly grin.

Steve, Richard, Frank, and Jason made their way back to the detention area. Unlike before, David didn't seem as angry. When he saw them approaching, he smirked and asked sarcastically, "What? A group visit this time? Pay me for the group show."

Richard ignored the comment and asked, "You said Liam was up to something last night. What was it?"

David leaned back lazily. "He was talking to someone important."

"Who?" Richard pressed.

David shrugged. "I don't know... but it was an important call. Doesn't this scene feel familiar?"

Richard frowned. "What do you mean?"

David grinned slyly. "Think hard about it."

Jason, overhearing, caught on. "*The Silence of the Lambs?*"

"Bingo!" David said with a chuckle.

Richard's frustration boiled over. "How can you joke about this?"

David just laughed. "Isn't it fun? When Liam was on the phone next to me, the student records were open."

Richard asked. "Did you see it?"

Jason leaned in, his voice tense. "Was it one of us?"

Richard cut in, his tone firm. "What do you want, David?"

David smirked. "Open the door first. Let me out."

Jason immediately protested, "No way!"

David's gaze sharpened. "Jason, think carefully before you speak."

Richard took a step closer. "Tell me whose name you saw, then I'll open the door."

David's smirk widened. "Do you think I'm a fool? Do whatever you want, but remember—my memory fades with time. I might forget that name."

The standoff ended in a stalemate. David refused to reveal what he knew, and the others weren't ready to release him yet.

***

Meanwhile, in her room, Eva struggled with her computer, unable to connect to the internet. Her frustration grew, but the others had far more pressing concerns.

***

Back in the hallway, Steve, Jason, Richard, and Frank debated their next move.

"Wait until Liam comes back," Jason suggested.

"And if he doesn't show up?" Richard countered.

"Another teacher will come," Jason insisted. "But we can't just let David out. For all we know, he could be involved in this whole mess. He might be working with the letter writer or worse—he could have hurt the teacher. The last person to see Liam is a major suspect."

Richard remained unconvinced. "You really think David would hurt someone? Liam knows judo—he can take care of himself. David is no match for him."

Jason argued, "That doesn't matter if someone hits you on the head."

Richard sighed. "Anyway, there are four of us!"

Jason dumbfounded by Richard's word. "Have you seen David fight when he's mad? The four of us? Forty of us wouldn't be a match for him!"

The conversation stalled, and Steve had had enough. He stood tall, his voice steady. "Alright, let's put this to a vote. If you think David should be released, raise your hand."

Richard, Frank, and Steve raised their hands. Jason scowled. "Wait a minute! We should ask the others—Eva, Angel, and Michael—for their votes too."

Steve shot Jason a look. "Just give up."

David's face brightened at the result. Without hesitation, he stood up and stretched.

"We're all dead now," Jason muttered.

Richard unlocked the door, and David stepped out. Steve immediately asked, "Whose name did you see?"

David grinned mischievously and leaned close to Jason. "Boo!" he teased, causing Jason to flinch. Laughing, David began to walk off, and the others followed closely behind.

"David, you promised," Richard reminded him.

Jason whispered to himself, "You really think mad David will keep a promise?"

They made their way to the teachers' dorm. Richard persisted, "Whose name did you see?"

David didn't answer immediately. Instead, he led them to the staff room, opened a drawer, and pulled out a file. He flipped through the student records leisurely until he found a page.

Richard, growing impatient, asked, "What are you looking for?"

Behind them, Jason muttered to Frank, "Stupid Richard! Why would he trust mad David?"

Finally, David stopped and smirked. "Here. It's not the name I remembered—it's the profile page I saw Liam looking at."

"Are you sure?" Richard pressed.

David tapped a smudge on the page. "I'm sure. I was eating cream bread last night when I saw it. Are we good now?"

Richard glanced at the student profile. The name read Tom Harris—1st year, Class 1.

"Same year as me," Richard murmured. "Do you remember him, Steve?"

Steve shook his head. "Not at all."

As David left the teacher's dorm, he mumbled under his breath, "That's Steve..."

Jason, standing by the door, stiffened. "Wait—'Pervert Tom,' right?"

Richard nodded, recalling the rumors. "Yes. He was the one who allegedly sexually abused Gary once."

Meantime, as David exited the school, Gary remained hidden, lying at the rafters above the main entrance of the male dormitory.

Back in the staff room, Steve, Richard, and Frank examined Tom's records further.

"It says here Tom took a leave in January," Richard noted.

Steve's eyes narrowed. "What day?"

"January 3rd," Richard replied.

"Right after the winter vacation," Steve said.

Jason asked, "Was it noted as an illness?" He noticed that an ambulance had been called to the school on Christmas Day, though no explanation was given.

"Did you give Tom that nickname—'Pervert'?" Richard asked.

Jason shook his head. "No, that's just what everyone called him."

Steve began searching the computer for class vacation call logs.

Frank asked, "What are you looking for?"

"Last winter, a teacher said two students stayed at school during the vacation," Steve explained. He checked the records and glanced at Richard. "Guess what? One of them was Tom."

Surprised Richard scanned the file. "It says here... Tom died on January 3rd."

The memory of the black letter flooded back to Richard. The ominous words echoed in his mind: *"After eight days, walk up the path by the tree. Under the clock tower, you will see someone dead."*

Richard looked up at the others, a sense of realization dawning on his face. "Tom meant that he would die," he said quietly. "We didn't receive just any letter—it was a suicide note. Last year's suicide note. Tom died, and that's what the letter was predicting."

Jason's voice trembled. "Then who sent the letter now?"

Steve's gaze hardened. "It must be his closest friend."

Richard's eyes drifted back to the student record. "According to this, it was Michael. Michael was Tom's closest friend." A heavy silence settled over the room as the truth sank in.

***

At the same time, Michael sat alone in his room. He stared intently at the peculiar photos he had taken of Eva after her suicide attempt, his fingers tracing the edges of the images as if searching for answers within them.

***

In the corridor, Richard, Jason, and Frank sat on a bench while Steve paced back and forth. Steve finally broke the silence. "Revenge for a dead friend... it makes sense. But it happened last year—why now?"

Jason replied. "Maybe he waited until the school was empty."

Richard said. "Why not tell the school or Tom's parents?"

Steve's expression became gloomy. "What if the principal knew but didn't take any action? The biggest donor's son was involved, and an unqualified teacher became permanent."

Jason nodded. "Yeah, that's why Cameraman Michael decided to take revenge himself."

Steve's gaze hardened. "But why did Michael send us a letter? What does he want from us?"

Richard considered it. "Maybe he feels someone died because of us. Maybe Michael wanted to make it known—to confront us with our own guilt."

Jason leaned back, looking satisfied. "That's it. Case closed."

Richard shook his head. "But something still feels off."

Steve agreed. "Yeah, there's more to this."

Jason rolled his eyes. "Why can't you make up your mind? Just go and ask him. If we rough him up a bit, we'll get the truth."

Steve remained unconvinced. He turned to Jason. "You don't know much about Michael, do you?"

Jason scoffed. "What do you mean?

Steve glanced at Jason, unimpressed. "I saw David smash Michael's camera before. Michael fought back, even though he got beaten afterward. And you, Jason—you could barely hold your ground against David, let alone a determined and angry Michael."

Jason's confidence faltered for a moment, but he quickly masked it with a glare.

Without another word, Steve turned away, heading toward the exit.

"Where are you going?" Richard called out.

Steve didn't look back. "I'll go outside and think."

Jason watched Steve leave, his irritation bubbling over. "What's wrong with Steve? Does he really think that cameraman Michael is better than me?"

Richard quietly got up and left, followed by Frank. Jason kept muttering to himself, "I left Steve alone because he's smart, but he's so clueless. Should I knock some sense into him?"

Meanwhile, back in David's room, Richard sat hunched over David's laptop, his eyes glued to the screen. Frank stood nearby, watching as Richard navigated through the CCTV footage.

"Who would've thought David's work would help us this much?" Frank said.

Richard's fingers paused on the keyboard, his gaze narrowing as he watched the screen. The footage showed Steve walking outside, his breath visible in the cold air.

Frank glanced at Richard. "What do you think Steve's thinking about?"

Richard snapped the tension evident in his voice. "How should I know?" The sharpness of his tone hung in the air for a moment before he exhaled slowly, composing himself. "Sorry. It's just... when I look at Steve I start to understand David a little more."

Outside, Steve had reached the clock tower. Snow crunched beneath his boots as he approached the dedication nameplate at its base. He leaned in, reading the inscription carefully: "Donated by President Miller (Gary's father), March 2024."

***

Jason had found Michael in the cafeteria. Michael was about to take his coffee from the machine when Jason, with a dark glint in his eye, snatched the cup.

"Thanks," Jason said smoothly.

Michael glared at him. "Don't look at me like that— we're friends, aren't we?" Jason added with a smirk.

Michael answered, "since when were we friends?"

"Friends," Jason repeated, almost tauntingly. "That's a nice word. So tell me, Cameraman Michael, who are your closest friends? If they're hurt, do you feel their pain? If they're beaten, do you beat the ones who hurt them? If they die... do you avenge their deaths?"

Michael's expression flickered, but he didn't answer. Before the tension could boil over, Richard stepped into the cafeteria, his timing sharp. He placed a firm hand on Jason's shoulder. "Jason, I need to talk to you," Richard said, pulling him away before things went too far.

Outside the cafeteria, Richard shot Jason a warning look. "We're just keeping an eye on him. We don't have any solid evidence against Michael, other than the fact that he used to be friends with Tom."

Relented Jason responded, "Fine. But if something happens, you're taking the blame."

Meanwhile, Frank continued to watch the CCTV footage. He saw Michael casually fiddling with the bookshelf in his room, seemingly unaware that the cameras tracked his every move.

***

David, on the other hand, was skiing his way down the mountain, determined to make it home despite the worsening snowstorm.

***

Later, Richard, Frank, Jason, and Steve entered Michael's room, searching through his drawers and bookshelves.

As they combed through his belongings, Richard made a disturbing discovery—Michael's books were filled with photographs of Eva.

At the School clinic, Michael had been lurking outside, watching Eva as she tended to Doctor John, who was suffering from a fever.

Michael had tried to sneak a photo, but the click of the camera against the glass door had betrayed him. Eva had turned sharply. "Michael?" she had said, startled.

Michael had slipped away before she could confront him.

Later, Michael returned to his room, only to find Richard, Steve, and Frank sitting on his bed, waiting for him. Jason slammed the door shut after Michael entered, trapping him inside.

Michael's face fell as he realized what was happening. "I feel locked up for some reason," he said.

Richard wasted no time. "We know who wrote the black letter," he announced flatly, his voice cold.

Michael's asked, "really, who?"

"Tom Harris! His nickname was Pervert Tom — do you remember?" Richard replied.

Michael's expression faltered at the mention of Tom's name. Jason added, "Of course you remember. Tom was your best friend."

Michael retorted, "Who said we were friends?"

Jason smirked. "Tom did. He already confessed, writing about a 'passionate friendship' with you."

"Don't lie," Michael shot back.

Jason pressed on, "Evidence number one: it's in the student records. Check it if you want. Tom listed you as his best friend. Here's the story — Tom was quiet, couldn't fit in at school. He got hurt by the innocent jokes his peers made. Every time that happened, he would've told you, his only friend. You tried to comfort him, but unfortunately, Tom died."

Michael's face showed genuine confusion. "Tom?" he whispered. "Did Tom die?"

Jason stepped forward. "Come on! You already know that."

Michael blinked, trying to process it.

***

Just then, a noise echoed from the clinic. Eva rushed inside, finding Doctor John struggling to stay on his feet, having knocked over some furniture.

"Doctor John, are you alright?" Eva asked, concern evident in her voice.

***

Back in Michael's room, Jason continued pressing. "Stop acting shocked. Just confess already."

Michael asked, "Confess to what?"

Jason snapped, "You sent the letters, didn't you? And you are trying to avenge your best friend Tom's death."

Michael shook his head firmly. "Jason, you have no idea what friendship is. Real friends are equals, without pity or sympathy. Do you even understand that?"

Jason scoffed, "Stop talking nonsense."

Michael replied calmly, "Tom listed me as his best friend in the school records. But I listed him as the person I disliked the most. You were a close second, by the way."

Richard's voice cut through. "You didn't like Tom?"

Michael's response was sharp, "of course not. He was the only one who completely treated me like I was some kind of disabled person."

Michael took off his hearing aid, his eyes burning. "I still remember Tom always asking if it was hard to adjust to life because of my hearing problem. He kept telling me I was strong, that I was great — but it sounded like he was saying, 'Be strong, Deaf boy!' I didn't need his pity."

Michael's voice wavered with bitterness. "What was worse was that Tom felt superior to me. I know everyone else thought the same, but no one made it as obvious as he did."

Jason interrupted coldly, "Even so, you're being a little harsh on a dead person."

Michael looked at him and said, "You followed me around and hit me, but I still preferred you over him — just barely."

Frank asked, "Then why did you hang around with Tom so much?"

Michael replied, "He kept following me around until I finally told him to get lost."

Jason, trying to regain control, pulled out the second piece of evidence — Michael's collection of photos of Eva.

Jason shook his head at the photos. "Even my mom didn't take this many photos of me. Tom also stalked Eva — friends with the same hobbies, huh? Just confess, Pervert Michael."

Michael shot back, "Taking photos of Eva isn't a crime. If it were, you'd be guilty too. I saw you hanging around whenever I took those pictures."

Jason bristled. Michael's ability to push buttons was relentless.

"You've got a secret crush on Eva, don't you?" Michael accused.

Jason's temper flared, his fists clenching. Just as he was about to lash out, the door swung open, and Eva stepped in, her voice urgent.

"Doctor John is running a dangerously high fever — his temperature is over 39°C. The internet and phone lines aren't working," she said.

Frank added, "It must be because of the snowstorm. They mentioned it on the radio."

Jason's eyes widened. "We're trapped now?"

Michael's face shifted, his attention turning to the situation. "If his temperature goes over 41°C, it could damage his brain. My hearing impairment happened because my mother had a terrible fever during pregnancy."

Richard immediately took charge. "We need to get to the clinic. Frank, stay here and keep an eye on Michael."

Frank nodded, his eyes never left Michael as the group left. He needed a break and excused himself to the washroom.

When Frank returned, his heart dropped — Michael was gone. In a panic, he checked the CCTV feed. On the monitors, he saw Michael casually walking toward the security office. In seconds, he bypassed the electric locks by pulling out the batteries, opening the door effortlessly.

Frank's breath caught in his throat as Michael disappeared inside. There were no cameras in that room.

Richard, Jason, and Eva entered the clinic. Richard approached Doctor John, who looked weak and feverish. "Did you take any medication?" Richard asked.

"Yes, about two hours ago," Doctor John replied wearily.

A little later, Frank entered the clinic and subtly signaled Richard to step outside.

Richard, who had been helping Doctor John by applying ice packs, turned to Eva. "Take the ice off him in a minute."

Eva looked at him, puzzled. "Where are you going?"

"To the library," Richard replied. "I need to see if there are any useful medical books."

Outside the clinic, Frank quickly explained what had happened with Michael. Richard's expression tightened.

"How did Michael get into the security room?" Richard asked.

Frank replied, "With the batteries."

"So much for the latest technology," Richard muttered. "What did he do inside?"

Frank shook his head. "There are no cameras inside the security room. I couldn't see."

They soon reached the security room. Richard immediately began inspecting the equipment. "The security computers seem fine, but the communication computers are down," he noted. He turned to Frank. "Where's Steve?"

Back in the clinic, Eva and Jason tended to Doctor John. The atmosphere was thick with tension.

Jason broke the silence. "Are you scared? Stuck here with six guys on a mountain and teacher is gone also?"

Eva arched an eyebrow. "Why? Are you planning to attack me?"

Jason's smirk wavered, his comment carrying a strange undercurrent. His next words were even more unsettling.

"Doesn't matter, I guess. You already tried to kill yourself once."

Eva said, "Why? If I'm going to die and since you have a crush on me, should you and I...?"

Jason replied in a childish, bitter sound. "Shut up."

Eva's gaze was steady. "Do you still like me?"

Jason hesitated. "Still, what do you mean by that?"

Eva's voice softened, almost distant. "Jason, maybe you were born kind. There's a reason you've turned out this way. But I'll never know what that reason is. You're just a loser to me."

"What are you trying to say?"

Eva's voice was calm. "That's the tragedy between us — the tragedy among all humans."

Eva turned and walked out, leaving Jason behind, his frustration simmering. "That psycho..." he talked to himself.

At the security room, Steve was bent over the equipment, his face twisted in frustration. Richard and Frank joined him, and Steve immediately started assessing the damage.

"The security computers are fine," Steve noted, "but the communication ones are completely down." He looked at Richard.

Eva soon arrived, she saw them. "Well, this is interesting. The smartest boy and the most obedient one breaking into the security room that Amazing."

Richard glanced at her. "How did you know we were here?"

Eva answered. "You're all acting suspicious. What's going on?"

Richard explained, "The phone and internet aren't down because of the snowstorm."

Steve held up a damaged circuit board, his voice heavy. "Someone sabotaged the communication mainframe. We can't even get a signal."

Richard asked, "Can you fix it?"

Steve shook his head. "I don't think so. The mainframe, graphic card, CPU — they're all fried."

Eva's mind raced. "Someone intentionally cut us off from the outside world? That's not good."

Later, Richard, Frank, Eva, Steve, Jason, and Gary gathered in the waiting area, sharing their suspicions.

Steve glanced at Jason. "You said the phones were down since morning. Michael went into the security room a little while ago."

Jason shrugged. "Maybe he went to check on it."

Steve still not convinced. "He knew the phones were down, Why he went there?"

Jason hesitated. "Anyway, it has to be Michael — Tom's friend, Eva's stalker, and a security room breaker. Who else could it be?"

Eva, unconvinced, interjected, "There's someone else."

Steve suggested, "The teacher?"

Eva nodded. "Liam. The sins listed in those letters are personal for us, but for him... if they come out, he could lose his job or even face jail time."

Steve seemed skeptical. "So?"

Eva's voice was steady. "What would you do if you were him? When cornered, people tell bigger lies to cover smaller ones. They commit bigger crimes to bury petty ones."

***

Meanwhile, deep in the snow-covered forest, David paused, his breath visible in the icy air. The wind bit at his exposed skin, and he tightened his grip on the beeping GPS in his hands — the only link to the outside world in this desolate place. Briefly, his mind wandered to the others, wondering what chaos might be unfolding back at the school.

***

Back inside the school, Jason's impatience boiled over. "We need to get out of here. We're stuck — we can't stay."

Eva frowned. "What about Doctor John? He can't go outside like this."

Jason retorted, "There's nothing we can do for him here. Let's go out and call an ambulance. Don't you think that's the better option?"

Steve immediately shot the idea down. "I'm not going. Even if the highway is clear, it will take at least five hours to reach there. It's already dark — if we leave now, we'll freeze to death out there. Staying here is our only chance."

Jason grumbled, "Still better than being stuck here with a lunatic." He turned to Gary. "What do you think?"

Gary shrugged indifferently. "I don't like walking long distances."

Eva cracked a half-smile, trying to lighten the mood. "I can't walk in the dark alone with a bunch of boys — my mom wouldn't like it."

Richard stood up, his expression firm. "We wait until morning. Doctor John's fever needs to drop first. Then we'll decide our next move. Tonight, we stay together — all of us, in the same room."

Steve suddenly spoke up. "The physics teacher was on duty last year, right?"

Richard said, "Yes, why?"

Steve didn't answer immediately. Instead, he began to walk off.

Richard called after him, "Where are you going?"

"To look for something," Steve replied.

"Take someone with you!" Richard insisted.

"I'll go," Frank offered, following after Steve.

As they left, Eva turned to Richard. "Where are the photos Michael took?"

"In my room," Richard replied. Then he turned to Jason. "Go check on Doctor John in the clinic."

Jason sighed, but he nodded and walked off.

Meanwhile, Eva made her way to Richard's room.

"It's better not to look at the photos," Richard warned.

"Why? Are they racy or something?"

Richard hesitated. "Do you really want to see them?"

"They're photos of me," Eva said firmly. She started flipping through the album. "Beasts that can't be understood... boys who are 18 years old."

A moment later, as Eva examined the photos Michael had taken of her, a disturbing thought crossed her mind: What did Michael do with these? Did he... masturbate? Geez!

Before the thought could take root, she ripped the photos from their frames, her hands trembling as she tore them apart.

"He's crazy!" she screamed. "I'm going to kill him!"

Richard quickly moved closer, trying to calm her down. "I'll get rid of those," he said, kneeling to pick up the scattered pieces.

As Richard reached down, his eyes caught something under the bed. His face tightened, and he grabbed Eva's arm, pulling her back just in time as Michael crawled out from beneath the bed, his expression startled and guilty.

Michael dropped a sharp object from his hands, his face pale. "Wait! Listen to me," he pleaded. He quickly grabbed the knife he had dropped. "Don't get the wrong idea. I came here to talk to you. I hid because you came here with Eva."

Richard's gaze hardened. "You were holding a knife."

"It's for self-defense," Michael replied quickly, desperation coloring his tone.

"From whom," Richard demanded.

Michael's eyes darted to the window. "You said the phones were down because of the snow. That's ridiculous. Look outside — do you see any power lines? No. Last year, during the school renovation, they made all the power lines underground, so snow couldn't have affected the phone lines. That means there's something wrong with the communications computers."

Richard's suspicion lingered. "Why didn't you say something earlier?"

Michael's jaw tightened. "All of you are already suspicious of me. What could I say? I needed to make sure first. We can't assume the communications computer broke down naturally."

Michael's gaze briefly met Eva's — a hard, unreadable look — before he turned and left the room.

***

Richard immediately checked Eva's room, ensuring everything was secure. "Will you be alright?" he asked.

Eva nodded, but her usual sarcasm was absent. "Yes."

Richard handed her a small whistle. "Lock the door. If anything happens, blow this whistle. I'll come running."

Eva's expression softened, a flicker of genuine gratitude breaking through her guarded demeanor. "Thanks."

Richard nodded, lingering for a moment before leaving. The door clicked shut, and Eva locked it behind him.

***

Outside, deep in the snow-covered forest, David's eyes finally caught sight of headlights glowing faintly from a distant road. Relief surged through him—a way out.

But his hope was cut short. As he shifted his weight, a sharp crack pierced the silence. David froze, his breath clouding in the icy air.

***

Inside the school, in the staff room, something unsettling was unfolding. Steve, with a look of intense concentration, poured over the physics teacher's calendar memos.

"The physics teacher always keeps notes on the calendar," Steve explained.

His eyes scanned the dates, searching for a hidden truth. Frank, quiet but attentive, lingered at his side like a shadow.

Steve's gaze locked onto December 25, 2023. The entry read: "Found Tom severely injured after he fell from the roof at the east wing."

Steve glanced at Frank. "Do you have the letter with you?"

Frank nodded, handing over the letter as they left the staff room.

Steve's voice broke the silence as he read the letter aloud. Each word hung heavy in the air:

"Jason tainted Tom and made him pitiful. Gary turned him into the monster in the corner. Liam silenced him. Eva ridiculed his false hopes. Richard took the only thing he had. Tom held out his hand, and Michael let go. I deleted him from my eyes."

Steve paused, his expression unreadable. Then, his gaze cut sharply to Frank.

"Did you transfer to Jasper High?"

Frank blinked, caught off guard. "What? Yeah, I did."

Steve questioned. "Did you take Tom's place after his death?"

Before Frank could answer, a sharp, frantic sound shattered the stillness—the piercing echo of Eva's whistle.

The boys sprang into action. Frank and Steve ran from the teacher's dorms, Jason bolted from the clinic, and Richard and Gary rushed from the male dorms. Their hearts hammered in their chests.

Outside, near the base of the school's fountain, they found Eva. She stood trembling, her eyes wide with fear, fixed on a spot before her. Her breaths were short and panicked.

Richard approached cautiously. "Eva... what is it?"

"Over here…" Eva stammered her voice barely a whisper. She pointed a shaky finger toward the base of the fountain. "Over here…"

The others followed her gaze. At first, they saw only a human hand half-buried in the snow. Then a cold wind swept through, brushing away the snow and revealing the rest—a face, pale and frozen. It was Liam.

His lifeless, barely recognizable face stared blankly, a grim testament to the danger that had been lurking. The group stood paralyzed, the weight of the scene pressing heavily on their chests. The horror was undeniable.

***

Meanwhile, miles away, David heard something else—a low, rumbling sound. He turned instinctively, his heart pounding.

The ground beneath his feet vibrated. A powerful, roaring sound filled the air, and realization struck him like a blow. An avalanche.

The mountainside trembled as a torrent of snow thundered toward him, an unstoppable force of nature. The roar was deafening, drowning out every other sound.

David's eyes widened with terror. His instincts screamed to run, but fear rooted him in place. The avalanche surged forward—a wall of snow, relentless and inevitable.

Chapter 4

One Lost, One Found

Michael stood in the kitchen, slicing vegetables. The knife glided smoothly through their soft flesh. He hadn't heard the sharp whistle that had sent the others rushing outside —his hearing aid was still in his room. In his quiet, oblivious world, the chaos outside was nonexistent.

Outside, Richard was the first to reach Liam's body. His boots crunched through the fresh snow as he approached. Kneeling, he checked for any signs of life. Jason's voice trembled.

"Is he dead?"

Richard nodded his expression grim. "Yes."

The body was cold, lifeless, and a thin trail of blood led away from it. As Richard stood, his boot hit something hard—metal. He bent down, picking up a knife. Its blade glimmered in the pale winter light.

Steve's voice cut in sharply. "I'd put that down if I were you. The police will probably check for fingerprints later."

Richard glanced at the knife for a moment too long before kicking it across the snow. The blade skittered away, catching the gray light.

Richard turned back toward the group. Their faces were pallid, shocked, as if they couldn't decide whether the body or the knife in Richard's hand had been more surreal.

Inside, Steve, Jason, Gary, Frank, Richard and Eva gathered. Eva's voice wavered. "Is he really dead?"

Steve squinted out the window, his breath fogging the glass. "It snowed before dawn. Liam must have died before then. The computers went down around that time—sometime between midnight and sunrise. Someone killed the teacher and cut us off from the outside world."

Frank's face twisted in confusion, "but why? Who would do that?"

Jason's voice was sharp, almost accusing. "I know who did it. Michael. He's the only one left who could've done it."

Frank stared. "What? Michael?"

As they filed into the cafeteria, they found Michael. He stood by the counter, his hands still sticky with vegetable juice and small cuts from the knife he had been using. The same knife now lay beside him.

Michael glanced up. "Where did all of you go?"

***

High in the mountains, a hiker in full gear spotted David's half-buried body, unconscious and pale from the avalanche. With care, she checked David's flashlight, noting the Jasper High label. Determined, she began to drag David's limp form onto a sled, pulling him through the snow with slow, relentless effort.

***

Back in the kitchen, Michael's gaze drifted over the group's tense expressions. "What's with you guys? Did you see a ghost?"

Steve muttered, "Something like that."

Michael chuckled nervously, "really? What? "I don't know what it was, but you must have witnessed it as a group. You all look so wan."

The group was silent. Michael's eyes narrowed slightly. The joking edge to his voice faded. Unnerved by the silent tension, Michael picked up his plate and started toward his room, the butcher knife still in his other hand.

Richard stopped him. "Are you going back to your room?"

"Yeah," Michael replied, a hint of frustration in his tone. "I feel like I'm choking here. I wanted to tell you something, but I guess now's not the time. See you later."

Richard's eyes fell on the knife. "Are you taking that with you?"

Michael paused, the blade still in his grasp. For a moment, it seemed like he might not let it go but finally, he set it down on the counter. Without another word, he walked out of the cafeteria.

Jason let out a slow breath. "Geez... This is so creepy."

Later, in the cafeteria, the group sat silently around the table. The weight of everything settled heavily on their shoulders. Jason leaned in toward Richard, his voice low. "You still think Michael's not the murderer? I'm sure it's him."

Richard hesitated. "I don't know."

Jason's frustration flared. "We saw Michael with the knife, asking us if we saw a ghost—we saw a dead body, for God's sake!" His eyes drilled into Richard. "What are you going to do about it?"

Richard blinked, caught off guard. "What do you want me to do?"

Jason's voice was fierce. "We get him first. Michael killed Liam—he could kill us all. We have to get him before he gets us."

Frank glanced nervously at the others. "Do you really think Michael did it?"

Jason snapped, "you idiot! Our suspect list was him and Liam. Now one's dead—it has to be the other!"

Eva muttered darkly, "You're polite now that Liam's dead. You always disrespected him before."

Steve went to the food counter, grabbed something for breakfast, and came to sit at the table.

Richard frowned. "How can you eat after seeing a corpse?"

Steve looked up calmly. "Aren't you going to eat?"

Gary clapped lightly.

Steve continued, "It's going to be a long night. We need energy. It's probably best if everyone eats something." He resumed eating without hesitation.

Later, in the clinic, Doctor John's fever burned hotter—40°C. His breaths were shallow, strained. Eva checked his temperature again.

Richard's concern deepened. "If it goes over 41°C, he could suffer brain damage. Do we have any fever reducers?"

Eva sighed, exasperated. "He can't swallow anything."

Richard's gaze hardened. "Crush it and mix it with water. Try to get him to drink."

Eva's frustration mounted. Not just from Doctor John's worsening condition, but the knowledge that there was a killer among them—possibly Michael.

Richard handed her a scalpel, its cold metal heavy in her palm.

"Take it," he urged.

Eva stared at the blade, unease tightening her throat. "Do you think I could stab him? If Michael comes, do you think I can do it? Would you be able to stab someone?"

Richard's eyes met hers, unyielding. "I will if I have to."

The calm certainty in his voice chilled her.

Moments later, Jason, Frank, Steve, and Gary entered, each armed with makeshift weapons—clubs, a baseball bat, a metal bar. Jason's grip on the metal bar was tight, his knuckles white. His eyes gleamed with determination.

Steve hung back. "Four boys should be enough for Michael. I'll stay here."

Jason's expression was fierce. "Let's go."

Richard turned to Eva, his voice a firm promise. "Stay here. I'll be back."

The group stepped out, weapons in hand, tension sharpening the air as they moved through the halls.

Jason, Frank, Gary, and Richard stood at the entrance of Michael's room. Richard, his voice calm but stern, warned, "Remember, we're here to catch him, not kill him."

Jason, his eyes burning with intensity, retorted, "We'll see about that."

Richard looked at him, exasperated. "Jason, we need to be humane in this situation."

"How can you be humane when you're faced with someone like him?" Jason replied, his grip tightening on the metal bar he held. "Let's see how you feel when a knife's pointed at you."

Richard knocked on the door. "Michael, we're coming in!" But the door creaked open, and they stepped inside.

Michael sat motionless in the dark, his back turned. There was no movement. No sound.

"Michael!" Richard called. "Turn around."

Jason squinted at the dark figure. "What's in his hand?"

Richard repeated his tone now firm, "Turn around."

When there was no answer, Richard began to count. "One…two…three"

At that moment, Gary by mistake, touched the light switch. The lights flickered briefly and then went out, plunging the room into complete darkness. Jason's heart pounded in his chest, and the next moment, panic overcame him. He raised the metal bar high above his head, swinging it with all his might. It crashed down with a sickening sound, but there was no cry, no resistance. Only the dull thud of metal hitting soft fabric, followed by a rustling noise—like feathers scattering in the wind.

Jason froze. His breath hitched in confusion. His hands trembled as he pulled the figure into the light.

It wasn't Michael. It was his clothes—stuffed with feathers and shaped to mimic a human form.

Gray apologized, hinting that he might've touched the switch button by mistake. "My bad!" he said quickly.

"My bad" Jason yelled, his voice a mix of anger and disbelief.

"I—I'm sorry, buddy!" Gray stammered, backing away.

They exited Michael's room in haste. The hunt continued, and the tension among the boys heightened with each step.

Back in the hallway, Jason's frustration boiled over. "Cameraman Michael, so you're hiding, huh? Stay hidden! You're dead if I catch you!"

Frank glanced at Richard. "Do you think Jason will be okay?"

Richard sighed, his voice low. "He's just scared."

Gary said "It's always the cowards who are the most violent."

***

Meanwhile, far from the chaos at the school, in the cold expanse of the mountains, David's eyes fluttered open. His head throbbed, but his body felt safe, wrapped in warmth. He shifted slightly, groaning as he became aware of the comforting embrace surrounding him.

The hiker who had saved him was still there.

"H-Hello..." David stammered.

***

Back at the clinic, Dr. John's fever raged on. Eva sat beside him, her hands trembling as she tried to feed him crushed fever reducers. His body bucked, rejecting the medicine as it spilled from his mouth.

Eva wiped his face, trying to keep him from choking on the vomit. Steve, sitting nearby, looked down at the map of the school, carefully jotting down notes on the clock tower's completion, the new main gate, and the timing of Tom's suicide attempt. The events were playing out in a meticulous order.

The door opened, and Jason, Richard, Gary, and Frank entered. Jason, his voice filled with frustration, spoke to Steve. "How could they not let us know? Mad David's been hacking the security cameras! They knew everything, and they've been enjoying the footage for themselves!"

Frank replied sharply, "We never enjoy anything."

Jason snapped, "Shut it."

Richard opened the laptop. Eva looked at him in confusion. "How can you hack into the system without internet access?"

Richard, calm as always, responded, "You can do it as long as the security system is still running."

Steve, who had been quiet until then, asked, "Where's Michael?"

Jason, gritting his teeth, replied. "We lost him! But don't worry, we'll destroy him."

Steve shook his head. "I'll be in the lab," he said, standing up.

Richard's gaze sharpened. "Why?"

Steve shrugged, "to make a rescue signal. There have been a lot of helicopters flying around recently. It'll be faster than walking out of here."

As Steve was about to leave, Jason shot him a look. "Aren't you scared? Michael's walking around with a knife."

Steve met his eyes, his expression steady. "You're the most dangerous person to me right now."

Jason sneered. "Whatever, you fool."

Richard interjected, "It's dangerous to go alone."

Steve turned to Frank. "Want to come with me?"

Frank, nodding, followed Steve to the school lab.

***

Meanwhile, in the mountains, David limped into the hiker's tent, wincing with every step. But his eyes brightened when he saw a young woman beneath all the layers of clothing. "Who are you?" David asked his voice hoarse.

The woman didn't reply. "Are you a soldier… or a spy?" he asked, his curiosity piqued.

The woman laughed softly. "No." David gave an awkward half-laugh in return, unsure of what to make of her response.

***

Back in the school's clinic, Richard, Jason, Gary, and Eva sat before the CCTV monitors. Jason was the first to spot Michael in Eva's room.

Without thinking, Jason bolted toward the Girl's Dorm. The others followed close behind.

When Jason threw open the door, Michael was just stepping out. The door slammed against the wall with a loud bang. Before Jason could even react, Michael shoved him aside with surprising strength.

"Get out of my way," Michael spat, his voice cold as he darted past Jason. The rest of the boys pursued him, hot on his heels.

But the chase didn't go as planned. Michael seemed to anticipate their every move, his escape calculated. He moved quickly, his steps precise, weaving through the school's corridors. The boys were losing him, but Jason refused to stop.

"Come out, Michael!" Jason shouted, his voice thick with menace as he stormed through the dark classrooms, dragging the metal pole behind him.

Michael, crouched beneath a desk, held a sharp weapon in his hand, poised to strike. But luck, or perhaps fate was on his side. Jason had entered the wrong classroom.

Michael remained hidden.

At the same time, Steve paced around the dimly lit lab, his hands fiddling with the tools laid out before him.

"Give me some tape," Steve asked Frank.

Frank passed him some tape, but his curiosity grew. "Is this a rescue signal?"

Steve looked up, his eyes intent on his work. "No, I need something else first."

Frank tilted his head, puzzled. "What's that?"

Steve paused for a moment before answering, "An electric shock device. I don't want to make it too strong, though."

Frank asked. "Where will you use it?"

Steve's expression was steady, "on you."

Frank blinked in confusion. "What?"

"I need to know why you sent the letters," Steve said, his voice calm but firm.

Frank's heart raced as he absorbed Steve's words. "How did you know?" he whispered.

Steve didn't flinch, "all the evidence points to you."

Frank's breath hitched. "What evidence?"

"The letter you sent," Steve said his tone flat. "It changed Tom's words."

Frank's face turned pale. "What do you mean?"

Steve continued. "'Walk up the path by the black spruce tree. Under the clock tower, you will see someone dead.'"

Steve paused for a moment before continuing. "But I think it was originally written like this: 'Walk up the path by the black spruce tree. Stand in front of the gates. You will see someone dead.'"

Steve continued, "Isn't that right? You can't see the east wing from the current gates, but Tom fell from the east wing, so you changed it to 'under the clock tower.' When Tom died, the clock tower hadn't been there yet—it was only after his death that they constructed it, along with the main gate."

Frank spoke, his voice cracking under the weight of years of unspoken pain. "My mother's number one goal in life was for me to get into Jasper High," he confessed.

"When I didn't pass the entrance exams, she cried as if the world was ending. I couldn't bear to see her like that. I ended up being the smartest kid in a regular school, the one everyone looked up to. But when I came here... it was like none of that mattered. I've become nobody. The people here... they're monsters. Sometimes, I wonder if I'm a ghost. I feel like I'm invisible. And what's worse is that I don't even know if I care anymore. Friends, Friendship, Does that even exist here, or is it just another lie we tell ourselves?"

Frank swallowed hard, his voice growing quieter as he continued. "A year ago, when I first got here, I ended up in Tom's room. It felt like... like I was stepping into his life. Into his skin, even. I didn't understand why, but I took his place. I found his diary there."

Frank's fingers tightened around the armrest of the chair as he relived the memory. "Tom wrote about how he didn't fit in; how lonely he was. It was like reading my own thoughts. I couldn't help it. I could empathize with his pain. It felt like it was happening to me. I don't think any of you ever knew whether he was even still here, whether he was alive or dead. But I knew his pain. And I wanted to make you all understand it—his pain, my pain. Do you understand?"

"No," Steve finally answered. "I don't."

Frank's face twisted in bitterness. "I guess that's not surprising. You don't even know anyone in your class."

Steve's eyes hardened slightly. "Maybe that's not such a bad thing."

Frank laughed darkly, "maybe not."

Frank looked down at his hands, the guilt weighing on him like a physical presence. "I didn't kill the teacher. I didn't break the communications system either."

Steve replied, "I know you didn't. You didn't have time—you were with Richard last night. He told me that."

Steve paused, asked, "Give me the gloves."

Frank questioned, "For what?"

"To make a rescue signal," Steve answered, now completely focused on the task.

Frank, his brow furrowed, inquired, "Who do you think killed Liam?"

Steve's expression was grim. "If Michael didn't have anything to do with the letter, it could be anyone."

Frank hesitated. "Are you going to tell the others that I sent the letter?"

Steve met his gaze steadily. "Do you think I should?"

Before Frank could respond, they both noticed something. Through the window, they saw Jason, Richard, and Gary walking outside, weapons in hands.

Steve turned to Frank, his voice steady. "They'll probably hunt you down."

Outside the lab, Richard, Gary and Jason arrived at the classroom, but Michael had slipped away again. After hours of searching, all their efforts to corner him seemed futile.

"Richard, you just saw him. Are you sure he came here?" Jason asked. Gary added, "Jason, You saw him too."

"Geez we should recharge ourselves and carry it around," Jason muttered.

As they left the classroom, Michael emerged quietly from his hiding spot behind the lectern. His gaze landed on the security camera, and a chilling realization dawned — they had been tracking him through the CCTV system. His every move was being monitored in real-time.

***

In the mountains, inside a small tent, a pretty hiker offered David a warm drink. "I still go rock climbing," she said with a gentle smile. "I even boxed for three years."

David glanced at her curiously. "Is that why you're out here alone for the rock climbing?"

She laughed softly. "In this case, it is ice climbing. What about you? Tell me about your school."

David hesitated, "my school?"

"The roads to the village are completely blocked," she explained. "We might face a second or third snowstorm. We may have to find shelter at your school."

David nodded slowly. "Okay."

***

Meanwhile, back at the school clinic, Jason, Gary, Eva and Richard watched helplessly as Doctor John's fever continued to climb. Richard checked his temperature — it was 41°C now. Jason absentmindedly tapped a metal bar against the ground, the clanging echoing off the walls.

Eva, desperate and exhausted, snapped, "Can't you stop that noise? You're so obvious. You can't sit still for a second. Are you that terrified of Michael?"

Jason face twisted with anger, "Michael? That heartless jerk! You wanted to die so badly that you slit your wrists. Michael should've killed you, not Liam. Don't you think so?"

His words hit Eva like a slap. Her expression hardened. "Michael said you're next."

Jason's rage flared. "If you want to die so badly, keep talking. I'll help you!"

Eva smirked bitterly. "Wow, thanks. I'll be sure to leave a message of your kindness in my dying breath — written in my own blood, signed, 'The Plague.'"

Before the argument could escalate, Richard stepped between them. "Enough," he ordered, his voice steady.

Jason yelled, "She started it."

Eva glared at him. "I'm going to my room."

Suddenly, Doctor John began to mumble, his feverish state growing worse. He started to sing a haunting lullaby, his voice wavering and delirious.

Richard quickly took control of the situation. "Jason, Gary, Eva — get some ice from the cafeteria. If there's none left, break some icicles. Bring Steve and Frank on your way back."

The plan was simple but desperate: a tub of ice to bring Doctor John's temperature down.

Meanwhile, Steve and Frank were still focused on the rescue signal when Michael appeared suddenly, a weapon in his hand.

Frank instinctively reached for his bat, but Michael was quicker, kicking it aside and leaving Frank defenseless.

In a swift move, Michael unplugged the security camera.

"Why is everyone doing this to me?" Michael demanded, his voice trembling. "Has everyone gone crazy? The Plague tried to burst my head open! What did I do? Is it because I took pictures of Eva? Is that a crime worthy of death? Fine, I get why Jason wants to hunt me, but Richard — of all people — has joined you?"

Frank stepped forward, his gaze steady. "Why did you kill Liam?"

Michael's expression shifted, a flicker of genuine confusion crossing his face. "Liam's dead? I couldn't have killed him... He was a judo athlete. How could I have...?"

Steve's voice cut in coldly. "Liam is dead, and one of us killed him."

"I don't believe it," Michael whispered, disbelief evident.

Suddenly, Jason entered the room. "Richard wants you at the clinic," he said, looking at Steve.

"Why?" Steve asked.

"The doctor's talking nonsense. He's driving us nuts," Jason replied.

"I'll be there in a minute," Steve answered.

Jason left, and Michael emerged cautiously from his hiding spot under the desk.

"He'll probably kill me one day," Michael whispered.

Steve looked at him. "Whether you killed Liam or not, there's a way for you to be safe."

In the school clinic's restroom, Richard prepared the bathtub, filling it with ice as Jason, Gary, and Eva returned, their arms laden with as much as they could carry.

"Richard, you're going to put him in a tub of ice?" Gary questioned, shocked. "Are you out of your mind?"

"What if he has a heart attack? It's dangerous!" Jason added nervously.

Richard's expression was firm. "My dad's a doctor. He taught me this — it's for patients who can't take fever reducers."

Uncertainty hung thick in the air, but Steve's voice broke through with a quiet resolve. "Let's just do it."

Together, they carefully lifted Doctor John and lowered him into the ice-filled tub. Richard instructed them to time three minutes as he performed CPR, his concentration unwavering.

Agonizing minutes passed, the room filled with tense, shallow breaths. When the time was up, they pulled Doctor John from the icy water and placed him back on the bed.

Richard frantically began drying the doctor. Eva, holding the thermometer, interrupted gently. "Richard... His temperature is still rising."

Jason sneered, the frustration bubbling over. "All that showing off, and it did nothing. He's still not getting better."

Richard's jaw tightened, his voice strained. "I'll take responsibility."

Jason snapped, "How? What's gone right since we started following your plans, Richard? If we had caught Michael earlier, we wouldn't be in this mess!"

Steve stepped in calmly. "Actually, I've already found Michael."

Jason, Gary, and Richard made their way to the detention cell, where Michael sat calmly behind the vantage wall steel door.

"What happened, Michael?" Jason sneered. "Did you surrender, camera man?"

Michael leaned back with a smirk. "Is that what you call trying to escape from a crazy dog? To be honest, if there were a murderer among the seven of us, wouldn't it be you? You have the closest profile to a criminal — violent, cowardly, and dirty."

Jason's grip tightened on the metal pipe he held. "What makes you think you're safe?"

Michael's expression remained cool. "How are you any different from a witch hunter?"

Frustrated, Jason pressed the metal pipe against the glass, desperate to get inside, but the vantage wall steel door held firm — unyielding. From behind its safety, Michael's smirk only grew. His laughter echoed off the cold walls, a sharp, grating sound.

Richard stood back, silent and contemplative, lost in thought. Even as Jason raged, Richard made no move to intervene. When the others left, Richard remained behind.

"Is this Steve's idea?" Richard finally asked his voice quiet.

Michael's smirk faded, replaced by a look of disappointment. "Richard," he said softly, "I'm really disappointed in you."

Jason stormed back to the clinic, his frustration boiling over.

"What do you think you're doing?" Jason demanded, glaring at Steve. "Did you lock Michael up, or are you protecting him?"

Steve met Jason's anger with a calm gazed. "As long as the person you think is guilty is locked up, you're safe. Isn't that enough?"

Jason fumed, his grip tightening on the metal bar. "What? What?"

Steve's voice remained steady. "What's the problem? You wanted to bash his brains out, but now you can't."

Jason's frustration found an outlet as he struck the metal bar against the wall, the clang echoing down the hall. Without another word, he stormed off.

***

Back in the detention cell, Michael watched Richard carefully.

"Do me a favor," Michael said quietly. "Show Eva the photos I took of her."

Richard's face hardened. "She already saw them. You were there."

Michael leaned closer Richard. "Show her properly, without letting your emotions get in the way. It's not that difficult. If you do me this favor, I'll forgive you for hunting me."

Richard hesitated, but the weight of Michael's words lingered. Finally, he took the photo album and headed to the girls' dormitory.

Eva opened the door her eyes squinted when she saw Richard standing there.

"Being at the girls' dorm this late — do you know how many demerits that is," she challenged.

Richard's voice was steady. "If you add up all my negative points, I'd be expelled anyway."

"What do you want?" Eva asked her irritation clear.

Richard held out the photo album. "Look at the photos."

Eva's eyes flicked to the album. "I already looked at them."

"Look once more," Richard insisted.

Reluctantly, Eva flipped through the pages. As her eyes moved over each photo, her face went pale. Tears welled up slowly, falling one by one until they became an uncontrollable stream.

"Are you okay?" Richard asked softly. "I'm sorry. I was wrong... Stop looking at it."

He reached out to take the album, but Eva clutched it tightly, refusing to let go. After a long silence, she finally spoke, her voice wavering.

"I think I was happy back then," she whispered. "I didn't know anything. I smiled. I don't know if I'll ever be able to smile like that again."

Her gaze drifted away, lost in memories. "Thank you. Tell Michael... I said thanks."

***

David lay awake in the tent, nerves prickling his skin as he listened to the quiet breathing of the girl sleeping beside him. His heart pounded in his chest, a mixture of fear and curiosity gnawing at him.

Summoning a shaky breath, he leaned over, his face just inches from hers. For a moment, he hesitated — then pulled back abruptly, retreating to his corner of the tent, his face burning with embarrassment.

***

The next morning at the school clinic, Frank gently wiped the sweat from Doctor John's face. Richard entered quietly.

"How is he?" Richard asked.

Frank glanced at the doctor, uncertainty in his eyes. "I don't know, but he keeps sweating."

Richard's expression softened. "When someone has a fever, sweating is a good sign."

Frank quickly checked Doctor John's temperature.

"Has it gone down?" Richard asked anxiously.

Frank showed the thermometer to Richard.

"It is 39°C now," Frank replied, a hint of relief breaking through his exhaustion.

Doctor John's fever had finally broken. Richard and Frank exchanged a glance, a quiet moment of triumph shared between them. They had saved him.

Meanwhile, Jason jolted awake in the room, his heart still racing from the nightmare. In the haze of his sleep, he had been desperately trying to explain, "Mom, it's not me. Mom..." But the words had faded as consciousness pulled him back, leaving him in a cold sweat.

At the same time, Richard made his way to the detention cell. Michael sat quietly inside, his expression unreadable. Richard handed over the photo albums.

"I'm giving these back to you," Richard said. "Eva told me to thank you. I looked at them again too. I don't know much about photography, but I can see that you genuinely like her."

Michael's eyes flickered, but he stayed silent.

Richard continued, "But it's not a justification for taking all those photos without her permission. I don't care if they led her to some grand self-realization—those hundreds of photos, especially the ones when she tried to commit suicide? That's not okay, Michael. It's not something you can just explain away with good intentions."

Michael finally looked up, a trace of defensiveness in his gaze. "Eva always photographs well, in every situation—from every angle. When she's mad, irritated, when she has no expression at all… even when she's hurting."

He unfolded one of his favorite photos, showing Eva's radiant smile. But as Richard looked closer, he noticed that Eva wasn't smiling at just anyone — she was smiling at him.

Michael's voice lowered, his vulnerability exposed. "You know Richard, why didn't I ever confess my feelings for her? The Eva I like... is the Eva with you."

Meantime, in the clinic, Frank pored over the security footage from the day Liam died. All he could see were two pairs of legs — a frustratingly partial view. Still, he tried to piece together what might have happened, re-enacting the possible events in his mind.

His concentration was broken by a surprising sound — Doctor John's voice. The doctor had finally woken up, his eyes fluttering open.

"Doctor John!" Frank exclaimed, moving quickly to his side. "Are you alright?"

Doctor John managed a weak smile. "I have no strength, but I feel... better."

Frank's relief was palpable. "Yesterday was... rough. I'll get you something to eat."

On his way to the cafeteria, Frank found Richard stirring a pot of porridge. As they prepared the meal, Frank shared his theory.

"Liam was stabbed from below," Frank explained. "That means the attacker's clothes would have blood on them."

Later, as Frank carried a bowl of porridge back to the clinic, he ran into Steve.

"How's the doctor?" Steve asked.

"Much better, his temperature is down to 37°C," Frank replied. "Did you finish the rescue signal?"

"Yeah," Steve nodded. "I'm going to try it out soon."

***

Richard found Eva outside, standing quietly over Liam's body. His face was so mangled it was barely recognizable. Eva's eyes were distant, a thoughtful, unsettled look in them.

"What are you doing here?" Richard asked gently.

Eva's gaze didn't shift. "Why did the killer take the knife out?" she murmured. "They usually leave it in the body, like in the movies. If the killer took the knife out, it must be because they wanted to hide the murder weapon. But then... why leave the knife nearby? And why smash Liam's face after stabbing him?"

In the clinic, Frank arrived with a bowl of porridge for Doctor John, only to find him struggling to put on his shirt.

"I'll help you," Frank offered, stepping forward.

As he helped pull the shirt over Doctor John's shoulders, Frank noticed a large, dark bruise on the doctor's back.

Doctor John caught the concerned look on Frank's face. "Is it that bad?" he asked quietly.

"Yeah... a little," Frank admitted. "Hang in there. We should be able to get out of here soon. Steve's made a rescue signal."

Doctor John managed a faint smile. As Frank served breakfast, the doctor inhaled the aroma. "Smells nice," he said his voice still weak.

Meanwhile, Steve found a lighter while searching through some belongings in the storage room. As he pocketed it, a crackling radio caught his attention.

The broadcast reported a chilling story — a series of murders at a girls' high school near Jasper High. An officer had been killed, and the suspect had fled, leaving a wrecked car at the bottom of a cliff.

Back in the clinic, Doctor John, still finishing his porridge, went to the medicine cabinet. He fumbled through it, grabbing something before sluggishly stepping outside. His movements were slow.

Doctor John encountered Jason in the hallway.

"Are you okay?" Jason asked, surprised. "I thought you were dying last night. Your temperature was over 41°C—they say you can get brain damage from that, but you're really lucky, you get better. And you weren't hurt in that car accident either."

"Yeah... I guess I'm very lucky."

"Where are you going?" Jason pressed.

Doctor John glanced away. "I was lying down for a long time. I just wanted to stretch my legs a bit."

As they walked in opposite directions, Jason called out, "Don't overdo it. You don't want to get sick again."

As Frank started to eat his breakfast, his mind wandered back to the bruise Doctor John had identical to the one David had shown them from Liam's judo throw. A terrible realization struck him. Panic setting in, he rushed back toward the clinic.

Outside, Richard knelt beside Liam's frozen body, brushing off snow and peeling back stiff, frozen layers of clothing. When he finally uncovered the wound, both he and Eva stared in shock. A gunshot wound.

At that same moment, Jason entered the empty clinic. Approaching Doctor John's bed, his metal pipe slipped from his grasp.

As Jason bent to pick it up, his fingers brushed against something tucked under the mattress — a bloody sweater, he pulled it out, realizing the implications.

Doctor John continued his agonizing climb up the stairwell, each step feeling heavier than the last. The ascent seemed endless, his breath ragged, but his resolve unwavering.

Finally, Doctor John reached the rooftop. Steve was there, crouched down, preparing to light the signal fire. The sound of helicopter blades grew louder — their rescue was near.

"Put that down," Doctor John commanded, his voice strained but steady. In his hand, he held a gun, aimed directly at Steve.

Steve stood slowly, his fingers lingered behind his back, still holding the fuse and lighter, attempting to ignite it without Doctor John's notice.

But Doctor John saw. His voice broke through the roar of the helicopter.

"I'm a mess, Steve. I'm tired. I've lost my patience. This is your last warning—put it down."

A smirk crossed Steve's face as he dropped the fuse and lighter.

Above them, the helicopter circled, its presence a stark contrast to the tension brewing on the rooftop.

***

From the mountain's peak, David and his savior gazed down at the school below. The helicopter's blades cut through the air, a sign of hope.

David grinned, his voice breaking the cold silence. "Okay! To a place where hot baths and coffee await! Let's go."

Chapter 5

The Black Letter Game

Doctor John stood motionless, his grip tight on the gun, the cold metal trembling in his hand. His voice was flat, emotionless.

"I'm a serial killer," he confessed, the words hanging heavily in the cold air. There was no plea for sympathy or forgiveness—just a raw, bitter truth.

"Five days ago, I was waiting for a taxi," Doctor John began, his gaze distant. "I was exhausted. Killing people, even those who deserve it... it's not thrilling anymore. I no longer felt responsible; it was just a routine. The taxi came, and as we were about to leave, the police appeared. They called my name, and in that moment, I understood. I was relieved—my mission unfinished, but I accepted my end."

Doctor John continued his voice steady but burdened. "I was being transported to prison. On the icy roads, the police car skidded off a cliff, crashing into the gully below. One officer was thrown from the vehicle, the other's head smashed through the windshield. I survived with just a wound to my forehead. Crawling from the wreckage, I saw a gun by the dead officer. The other officer, still breathing, tried to move, but I didn't hesitate. I shot him in the head."

Doctor John's eyes glazed over lost in the memory. "Wandering through the snow, I thought about ending it there. I held the gun to my head, ready to pull the trigger. But through the blizzard, I saw a light—Jasper High. Something inside me shifted. That light brought me to all of you, and I didn't know that every event had meaning. I realized all the coincidences were pieces of a fate laid out. So, I began my journey toward your school."

Doctor John eyes refocused on Steve. "Should we go back down?" he asked, his voice suddenly composed.

Meanwhile, inside the school, Richard and Eva returned from examining Liam's body.

"Liam wasn't stabbed with a knife," Richard muttered. "So why was it there?"

"To hide the real weapon" Eva suggested. "But if they wanted to hide the weapon, why leave it out in the open? It would've been smarter to hide the body altogether."

"Unless the killer couldn't hide it," Richard replied.

Their conversation was interrupted by Frank, breathless and frantic.

"I have something to say," Frank blurted out.

"What is it?" Richard questioned.

"Remember the bruise on David's back?" Frank asked.

"Yeah," Richard nodded.

"Doctor John has the same bruise—from his shoulder to his waist. I saw it earlier. On the CCTV footage, I couldn't see faces, but I saw Liam throwing the murderer to the ground before he died."

At that moment, Jason appeared, holding a blood-soaked sweater.

"This was under Doctor John's bed," Jason said, his voice trembling.

The realization hit them all simultaneously.

Upstairs, Steve and Doctor John entered the detention room where Michael sat, his expression wary.

"What's this about?" Michael asked his voice cautious.

Doctor John's gaze was sharp. "We came to open the door for you."

Michael's eyes narrowed. "I can go out? What about Jason?"

"We know who killed the teacher," Doctor John replied calmly.

Michael's curiosity got the better of him, "really, who?"

Doctor John's reply was chilling. "Be patient. You'll find out soon enough."

The door clicked open, and Michael stepped out, his eyes darting nervously.

"Is it one of us?" he asked.

Doctor John's gaze hardened. Slowly, deliberately, he raised the gun and pointed it at Michael.

Meanwhile, Panic set in as Richard, Eva, Frank, and Jason ran toward the detention center.

"Where are you going?" Frank asked desperately. "We need to find Doctor John!"

"No," Richard said firmly. "We need to gather everyone first."

Just as they reached the hallway, they found Steve and Michael approaching.

Richard's eyes widened. "Steve, did you release Michael? Where's Doctor John?"

A cold, calm voice answered behind them. "Are you looking for me?"

Doctor John stood there, his expression unreadable, the gun still in his hand.

Doctor John herded everyone into the waiting room—Jason, Richard, Steve, Frank, Michael, and eventually Eva. He sat at the front, his gun resting on his lap.

"Is everyone here?" Doctor John asked.

Jason looked around and frowned. "No, we're missing someone."

Doctor John demanded, "Who?"

"Gary," Jason replied.

Unbeknownst to everyone, Gary sat hidden in the rafters above, his headphones on, lost in his own world, oblivious to the chilling confrontation below.

Eva, her hands trembling, brought tea for Doctor John. He accepted it with a weary smile.

"Thank you, Eva," he said softly, taking a sip.

As she took a seat, Doctor John spoke again. "I'm so tired—I hope I don't pass out again. Oh, and I should thank you all for last night—especially you, Richard. I know you saved my life. I'm genuinely grateful."

Richard's jaw tightened, his eyes burning with restrained fury.

"Don't be that way," Doctor John chided lightly. "Everyone deserves treatment—friend or foe. Isn't that what you've learned?"

Frank asked Doctor John why he killed Liam. Doctor John explained, "Liam's death was a tragedy. I didn't want to kill him, but after he heard the news on the radio, he started asking me questions. He began to suspect me. Sooner or later, he would have realized it was me who killed the police officers after the accident. I couldn't risk being exposed, so I killed Liam to keep my secret safe. I hope you can understand." Doctor John sighed, his voice hollow.

Richard's response was firm and cold. "You killed someone. How can we understand that?"

Doctor John replied, "Think of it from my perspective; then you will understand..." He pointed the gun at Jason, who instinctively flinched.

Doctor John continued, "As you can see, I'm not feeling well. I'm sensitive, not as generous as I usually am, so don't try anything stupid. Can you understand that?"

Jason put his hands up and nodded.

***

Meanwhile, outside the school, David and the mysterious hiker girl stumbled upon a sign. They were just a few miles from Jasper High. They exchanged relieved smiles, celebrating their proximity to safety.

***

Back inside the school, Doctor John wasn't finished. "We're going to find the lost sheep. We may lose many sheep trying to find that one, but we still have to try."

Doctor John wanted to ensure no one would attempt to escape, so he paired up the students, deciding that only one from each pair would be sent to search for Gary.

"Steve, Frank—group one. Michael and Jason—group two. Richard and Eva—group three," Doctor John ordered. "One person from each group will leave to find Gary. The rest of you will stay here as hostages. If Steve doesn't return, Frank will be punished, and the same goes for the rest of you. It's really simple—it's not hard, right?"

Frank hesitated. "What is the punishment?"

"We will see about that," Doctor John responded. "Those who will search: Richard, Steve, and Michael..."

Jason whispered, "No way."

Doctor John continued, "Richard, Michael, Steve—leave and seek your departed friend now."

"What if we don't find him?" Steve asked nervously.

"I haven't thought about it," Doctor John replied. "I know the school is big, but I'm sure you'll find him—unless you don't look for him on purpose. You'll find him for sure, right? You have thirty minutes. Meet back here with Gary."

Jason muttered, "You know they won't come back. They could just hide."

Doctor John replied, "Jason, it's a little unfair to the hostages, so I've prepared this part—last words from the hostages. Beg or ask them to come back. Let's begin with Eva."

Eva remained silent.

"Eva," Doctor John prodded. "Don't you think you trust Richard too much? I know Richard is a good boy, but think of the situation at hand. You tried to kill yourself too. Richard might think, 'Eva tried to die, so she will understand.' What if Richard thinks that way?"

Eva remained silent.

"Silence is a good message too," Doctor John commented.

Richard said gently, "Don't worry, Eva."

Doctor John turned to Jason, "your turn now."

Jason responded, "This is stupid."

"Is that all?" Doctor John pressed.

Jason looked at Michael. "Michael... you will come back, right? I'm sorry about yesterday, but the situation—you understand, right? It wasn't just me; everyone felt the same way…"

Doctor John interrupted, "Frank, you're next."

Jason continued desperately, "I know I'm bad, but I don't deserve to die. You'll come back, Michael, right?"

"Enough!" Doctor John barked.

Michael looked at Jason and said, "What would you do?"

"Frank, your turn now," Doctor John insisted.

"I'm sorry," Frank whispered.

"Don't forget—ten o'clock," Doctor John reminded them.

Doctor John observed Steve and Richard exchanging subtle glances and suddenly changed his mind.

"Wait," Doctor John said. "Let's have Frank go. Steve, you stay here." Steve reluctantly sat down.

"Your time starts now. I'd hurry up if I were you," Doctor John said.

The clock was ticking. Richard checked the CCTV footage in his room but couldn't see Gary. Meanwhile, Michael and Frank had searched nearly every corner of the school. Desperation weighed heavily as the minutes slipped away. Despite searching every hallway, classroom, and storage room, Gary was nowhere to be found.

Back at the waiting area, Doctor John, still holding his gun on the remaining hostages, noticed Steve's agitation.

"Why did you switch us?" Steve demanded. "You didn't think I would return."

"Instinct," Doctor John replied coldly. "A signal went off in my head. It told me it would be dangerous to send you."

Jason glanced at the clock, sweating.

Doctor John smirked. "How big is the space that separates life and death? I was going to kill that taxi driver just before the police caught me. How big was the space between life and death for that driver? What about for you now?"

Jason's eyes locked onto the clock, terror setting in.

"It's almost Time." Doctor John said. "Should we start the countdown?" He began, "9... 8... 7... 6..."

Frank returned. Doctor John continued, "5... 4..." Richard returned.

Doctor John's gun remained trained on Jason as he counted, "3... 2...1." He clicked the hammer of his handgun.

At the last moment, the door burst open. Michael rushed in, breathless and wide-eyed.

Jason sagged in relief—he had been moments away from death.

***

Outside the school, David and the hiker girl trudged steadily toward Jasper High, their progress slowed by the raging snowstorm. The blinding snowflakes stung their faces, and the cold seeped deep into their bones. Despite the harsh conditions, they pressed on, determination written across their faces.

A brief moment of levity came when they paused for an impromptu snowball fight. It was a rare break from the intensity of their journey, laughter breaking through the heavy silence that had settled around them.

***

Inside the school, however, the tension was far from over. Doctor John, still gripping the gun tightly, fixed his gaze on Richard, Michael, and the others. His mistrust was clear.

"You didn't find Gary, then?" Doctor John asked, his voice cold and calculated. "Couldn't find him... or didn't want to? Or maybe you found him and hid him?"

Richard, trying to stay calm under the pressure, replied, "If Gary didn't want to be found, it would've been nearly impossible. This place is huge."

Doctor John's eyes darkened as his grip on the gun tightened. He stepped closer, his voice growing more dangerous. "You could be right... That's true. Then what should we do?" he asked, his tone chilling. "Not all the players are here, and we can't start the game."

Steve, unsure of what Doctor John was talking about, asked, "What kind of game?"

Doctor John's lips curled into a faint, unsettling smile. "A game I was really looking forward to," he said, his eyes never leaving the group.

Richard's jaw clenched. "We didn't agree to any game," he shot back.

Doctor John's gaze shifted coldly between the group. "You did when you welcomed me to your school," he said, his voice like ice. "Now, what should we do? Forfeit the game, or just a little penalty?"

Suddenly, his gun shifted, the barrel aimed at Richard. "The leader?" Doctor John's voice was dangerously calm as he moved the gun from Richard to Steve. "The ace player?" Finally, his gaze fell on Eva. "And the player with a problem... pretty girl makes a good sacrifice."

His words were deliberate, measured, and the room fell into an eerie silence. Doctor John was in control, and he knew it.

"One of you will be the sacrifice," he declared, his voice low but firm. "That's how it works."

Richard's anger boiled over. He stood abruptly, shaking with fury. "Are you insane? What game? What sacrifice? Do you think holding a gun makes you a god? You're just a murderer!"

The words tumbled from his mouth, his fists clenched as he took a step forward. He was ready to attack, to put an end to this madness, but Doctor John was faster. The gun was aimed at Richard's head in an instant.

"I'm disappointed," Doctor John said coldly, his voice steady. "Someone who displays hostility is so easy. But I'm not doing this for fun, either. If the first rule isn't followed, the game can't be played. If you want, Richard, I can give you the penalty." He pushed the barrel of the gun against Richard's forehead. "Is that what you want?"

The tension in the room was suffocating, every breath a struggle. Just as the situation reached its breaking point, a noise came from above. Everyone froze, eyes darting toward the ceiling.

To their shock, Gary casually descended from the rafters, his movements effortless and deliberate. Doctor John chuckled. "Our goose was right above us," he said, shaking his head in disbelief.

Later on, it was breakfast time, and Gary sat next to Doctor John, handcuffed to the table—a silent witness to the strange ritual unfolding around him.

Eva, Steve, and Frank were busy preparing breakfast plates with toast, eggs, and more. Richard and Michael sat in front of Doctor John, their eyes flicking nervously between each other and their unsettling host.

As Eva set down a plate, her eyes lingered on one of the knives on the table. Her fingers twitched subtly, a hint of temptation. Steve, sensing her intent, moved casually past her, deliberately bumping into her shoulder, breaking her concentration. The moment passed, and the group gathered around the table to eat.

Richard looked at Doctor John. "You said you want to play a game, what kind of game?"

Before Doctor John could respond, Gary's gaze fell on the gun at his side. "Is that a real gun?" he asked.

Doctor John's smirk widened. "Okay, it seems like there are a lot of questions floating around. How about this: Let's have a question-and-answer session. Each of you can ask me a question, and I promise to answer truthfully." His voice was calm, detached, as though they were having a casual conversation.

Steve spoke up. "Can we discuss the questions before asking?"

"No," Doctor John replied flatly. "Who should we begin with? Gary, is your question about the gun?"

Gary hesitated before asking, "How many people have you killed?"

"Eight, including your teacher Liam," Doctor John replied without a hint of remorse, "

A heavy silence fell. When it was Eva's turn, she asked, "Why did you kill those high school girls?"

Doctor John's expression remained blank. "They were impolite, so loud and offensive. They swore, they laughed... it bothered me. I can bet you this—the people on the bus that day probably felt the same way I did. They probably thought, 'I wish those girls would disappear.' So I thought about it. Those girls living on, carrying on with their lives was that beneficial? Apparently not, so I killed them."

The room went cold. No one spoke, paralyzed by the brutal simplicity of his confession. Steve, the only one seemingly unaffected, continued eating.

Richard asked again. "What is the game you plan to play with us?"

Doctor John leaned back, his eyes glimmering with amusement. "Remember the letters you all received? The game is simple. It's a race to find the Black Letter Sender. If you figure it out first, I'll punish the sender. If I find out first, I'll punish the person with the worst 'black letter sin.'"

Jason asked nervously, "What if the sender confesses?"

Doctor John's smirk tightened. "If the sender confesses... I still win."

Jason muttered, "That's not fair."

"Isn't it?" Doctor John countered smoothly. "But life itself is unfair."

Michael, wary, asked, "How will you find out who sent the letter?"

"You can use any method you want to find the sender," Doctor John said casually. "But I'll be conducting one-on-one counseling sessions with each of you. Think of it as therapy—I'm just a counselor, not a torturer."

Doctor John's gaze landed on Steve. "Your turn, ask your question."

Steve considered before asking, "How many bullets do you have left?"

Doctor John's smile lingered. "Four. I had six. The first was a warning, the second... killed Liam. Worst case scenario, three of you will live."

Doctor John then led the group upstairs to the last floor hall. Standing behind them, gun in hand, he announced, "We'll start the sessions now. Relax until it's your turn."

Michael asked, "What if we lie during the session?"

Doctor John chuckled softly. "I don't mind. A good counselor finds more truth in lies than in honesty."

Doctor John glanced at Michael. "Michael, you stay here. The rest of you, go inside."

With everyone locked in the teachers' dorm, Steve began searching frantically. Frank asked, "What are you looking for?"

"Anything we can use as a weapon," Steve replied urgently. "It's our only chance."

Richard tried to open a window, but it was firmly shut.

Steve's gaze hardened as he looked at Richard. "Why did you come back before?"

Richard blinked, confused. "What?"

"If all three of you hadn't come back, Doctor John wouldn't have known what to do," Steve muttered. "Four of us including Gary hiding would have been harder to control."

Jason questioned Steve's confidence. "How do you know? Doctor John is a lunatic."

Eva added thoughtfully, "Maybe Steve's right. Doctor John picked the pairs carefully to make sure they all returned."

Frank frowned. "I get why he paired you with Richard, but Michael and Jason? That doesn't make sense."

Eva shook her head. "Doctor John knew they couldn't get along. Michael hates Jason, if Michael had left Jason behind he would've died. And Doctor John knew exactly how to manipulate that. For Michael, running away wasn't just escaping—it was the same as murder."

Meanwhile, in the clinic, Doctor John handcuffed Michael to the bed, placed his gun on the table, and sat across from him with a diary and pen. "Why does everyone call you 'Cameraman Michael'?"

At the same time, in the boy's dorm hall Jason questioned aloud, "Why Michael first? It can't be random. If Doctor John was that careful in picking pairs, he wouldn't pick just anyone as the first session."

Frank asked, "Then why Michael?"

Jason's face tightened. "Doctor John knows Michael sent the letters."

Richard groaned. "Not this again!"

Jason admitted that he misunderstood Michael. "I made a mistake thinking Michael killed Liam. But he's the only one connected to Tom. Doctor John doesn't have proof—just a hunch. I am sure Doctor John trying to talk Michael into a confession. 'I'll let you live, just admit it'—it's a ridiculous game."

Eva whispered to Jason, "Thank goodness you didn't send the letters. You'd confess before he even asked."

Jason shot back, "Wouldn't you? Would you be willing to die for everyone else?"

Eva claimed. "Maybe I wouldn't, but at least I'd think twice about it."

Jason scoffed. To him, there was no difference between them.

As the group's fear and suspicion grew, Frank quietly wrestled with his guilt. He knew the truth—he had sent the letters.

The weight of his secret bore down on him, yet he found solace in Steve's guarded but steady presence.

Steve's poker face could fool anyone, but Frank knew there was a good heart beneath that cold exterior.

In the sterile, cold room of the clinic, Doctor John had handcuffed Michael to the bed. Yet, Michael's tongue was freer than ever — a relentless, compulsive chatter that filled the space.

"Are you going to write a book later on?" Michael asked, a sly smile curling on his lips. "Most serial killers do it in prison. They sell the rights for a huge sum, and a film gets made. The killer becomes rich, but there's a law now. If they make money from books or films, it all goes to the victims' families. You know, everything's so exaggerated in the movies. I love movies..."

Doctor John quietly noted Michael's behavior as "compulsive gossiping."

Meanwhile, in the teachers' dorm room upstairs, Richard and Steve sat together, tension hanging between them. Richard leaned in, his voice barely a whisper.

"Is there a way to get out this situation?"

Steve hesitated. "Yes, there are few ways, but I don't know if it will work."

"The faster, the better," Richard pressed. "He's a psychology expert. The longer this takes, the more disadvantaged we are. Michael's alone with him now — it makes me nervous."

"I don't know about that," Steve admitted, "but I agree we need to act quickly. As time goes on, he'll learn more about the system of our school."

Richard's eyes sharpened. "How fast, then?"

"Tonight."

Together, they began formulating a plan with whatever they had — a few household cleaning agents and a handful of desperate ideas. The decision was made: tonight, they would act.

Back in the clinic, Michael's monologue continued without pause. "Brad Pitt kills the photojournalist at the end of that movie. I guess directors don't really like journalists. Look at Die Hard 1 and 2 — journalists are always shown as pests."

"Michael," Doctor John interrupted firmly.

Michael continued, unphased. "Have you seen it? Bruce Willis, right?"

"Michael!" Doctor John's voice was sharper.

"Yes?" Michael replied innocently.

Doctor John, overwhelmed, sighed and requested, "Five minutes of silence, please."

Michael blinked, taken aback. "I see... Am I going on and on? Sometimes words just flow out of my head like a waterfall..."

"Shhh!" Doctor John insisted, taking a measured sip from his cup. Silence finally settled.

Michael fidgeted, his fingers tracing the edges of his ears until Doctor John spoke again. "You're a good storyteller, you know," Doctor John began. "You know how to start strong, how to change topics, and you sprinkle in humor. But I can't laugh because you seem so desperate."

Michael's smile faded slightly. "The current situation..."

"Yes," Doctor John cut in. "You must be nervous. As you said, it's not often you sit with a serial killer. You know there's a moth called Rhasastic mongoliana. It has a decorative pattern that looks like a snake from above, so birds avoid it. It uses its most vulnerable trait as a defense mechanism. Do you know why the way you talk sounds so desperate? Because it's your camouflage. Listening and talking—does your disability still burden you?"

Michael's face fell. Doctor John's words cut deeper than expected. Tears welled up, his defenses momentarily shattered.

***

Meanwhile, David and the Hiker were trudging through the snow toward the school. As they ate, the girl asked, "How much further to your school?"

"I don't know," David said. "I don't have any sense of direction or distance in this snow."

David noticed a pendant around the Hiker's neck and asked, "What kind of jewel is that?"

"It's a gallstone," she replied simply.

"A gallstone? From inside your body? That's... weird. Is it yours?"

"It's just a lucky charm," she said softly. "To protect me."

David tilted his head. "Do you get afraid of things? Ghosts?"

She replied quietly, "Headaches."

David shrugged. "You should take some medicine for that."

***

Back in the clinic, Michael's voice filled the room once more.

"When I was six, our preschool put on a music show. I was in charge of the cowbell — just one shake at the end of the first verse and another at the end of the second. It was nothing compared to the castanets or tambourine. My dad videotaped it. There were fifteen of us on stage, but I stood out from the group. I was standing just like everyone else, but my face was the only one that was different. You said I was desperate. That's how I looked back then... desperate. It was nothing special. No one would have cared if I didn't ring it. I was so nervous—I kept looking around."

Michael painted that moment as the worst of his life.

"That's what it means to be disabled. It's nothing to anyone else, but to me... I'm really desperate," Michael said, his voice low.

Doctor John, never missing a beat, asked if Michael remembered whether he had rung the cowbell or not.

Michael lied, claiming he didn't remember. But Doctor John knew better.

In the other room, Richard, Steve, Frank, Jason, Eva, and Gary gathered around a table cluttered with a flammable spray can and a lighter. Steve took charge, his voice steady.

"The only place we can predict Doctor John's movements is the cafeteria. He'll sit there at lunch. Someone will sit close, and the rest will be in front of him. When he puts the gun down to eat..."

At that same moment in the clinic, Doctor John began another analogy.

"Have you seen animal documentaries, Michael? When there's a drought, thousands of zebras gather at the river. A lion waits there, but it's only after one zebra — the weakest, the injured, the one separated from its mother. It's not just the lion that waits for such a zebra; the other zebras wait too. They want the sacrifice to show itself quickly so they can drink safely. Imagine you're that injured zebra, but no one knows it — not the lion, not the others. What would you do?"

Michael hesitated. "Why are you asking me that?"

"Because the lion by the river and your situation are quite similar," Doctor John replied calmly.

Satisfied with the silence that followed, Doctor John smiled softly. "Alright, should we finish up?" Then, he tossed a key to Michael.

In the other teachers' dorm hall, Steve crafted a makeshift bomb, hiding it near the ceiling — a desperate measure born of fear and frustration.

Later, Doctor John led Michael to the teachers' dorm where Steve, Richard, Eva, Frank, Jason, and Gary were locked up. Michael opened the door and joined them.

Doctor John ordered them to walk hand in hand toward the cafeteria. He followed them, a strange procession of captives and captor.

Michael struggled to follow Doctor John's words without reading his lips—his hearing issues made it difficult.

Richard whispered something to him, but Michael couldn't understand.

When they arrived, Michael sat to Doctor John's left. Frank and Eva busied themselves preparing lunch while Steve, Jason, Gary, and Richard took their seats in front of him.

Steve broke the silence first. "Did the session go well?" he asked.

Doctor John took a measured sip of water before answering. "Yes, thanks."

Steve leaned forward. "What did you discuss?"

Doctor John smiled faintly. "Psychologists and priests must keep their clients' privacy."

Steve, quick and composed, shifted the conversation. "What happens if there's a tie in this game? What if neither we nor you find out who sent the letters? How does that work?"

Doctor John's expression darkened slightly. He leaned in. "Then I lose, generous, right?"

Doctor John exhaled slowly before continuing. "To be honest, the only way I win is if the sender confesses." His voice dropped lower, colder.

"To the sender—if you stay silent, you can protect everyone. But you have to trust the others won't give you up. And to the other six of you—if you figure out who sent the letters, you may choose not to tell me. But again, you have to trust that the sender won't break under pressure and confess."

Doctor John studied their faces. "Yes, trust is the basis of this game. How much do you trust each other? You are the smartest in this country. Has anyone ever taught you about trust?"

At the same time, Steve's plan was beginning to take effect. A small flame flickered to life in the other hall, near the ceiling.

Frank and Eva returned, setting plates of food in front of everyone. They ate in utter silence, the tension thick enough to cut. Richard and Steve exchanged glances, waiting for the moment.

Michael sat off to the side, his mind drifting. His hearing aid malfunctioned, leaving him isolated in the white noise of chaos.

Doctor John tapped his fork against the table. "Strange," he mused. "I didn't expect this meal to be enjoyable, but I didn't think it would be this tense. What is it?"

Before anyone could respond, a sudden explosion rocked the building. Steve's makeshift bomb had gone off.

The fire alarm blared, drowning out everything. Students leaped to their feet in panic, chairs screeching against the floor.

"Get the gun!" Richard shouted, turning to Michael. But Michael couldn't hear him. He could only see the panic in their eyes, the desperation in their movements—but he didn't know the plan.

Richard hurled a drinking glass at Doctor John before lunging over the table, reaching for the fallen gun. But he was too late.

Doctor John, faster and more precise, seized the weapon in a single motion, pointing it directly at Richard's head.

Michael's heart pounded. He could only watch in slow motion, too late to act, too late to stop it.

The fire alarm abruptly shut off.

Doctor John began to laugh. "When the police caught me, I thought it was over. But the snowstorm, the accident, and even now… It seems fate is on my side."

Eva, Steve, Jason, Frank, Richard, Gary, and Michael stood in front of him, the gun trained on them.

Doctor John continued, "Why? Why does fate favor me? That was close, right? Anyway, we need to wrap this up. What should we do?"

Doctor John's gaze landed on Jason, the weakest among them. He aimed the gun. "Let's try to guess who planned this. I'm pretending to be calm, but my adrenaline is pumping. I didn't get to eat dinner, and I almost smashed my forehead. Do you think I'll tolerate silence in this situation?" He smirked. "Tell me, Jason. Who orchestrated this?"

Jason hesitated, his eyes darting around the room.

"Why are you asking me?" he stammered.

Doctor John ignored him and began counting down. "Five… four… three…"

Jason panicked. "Ask someone else!"

"Two…"

Under the pressure of the gun's muzzle, Jason cracked. "Steve! He started it!"

Doctor John's eyes gleamed with satisfaction. "I knew it."

He swiftly handcuffed Steve and left him behind, forcing the others to march out of the cafeteria.

Outside the teachers' dorm, Richard's voice cracked with desperation. "What are you going to do with Steve?"

Doctor John's voice was calm, almost indifferent. "Shouldn't it be a life for a life?"

Richard's breath hitched. "We didn't want to kill you. We just wanted to take your gun."

Doctor John tilted his head. "And once you had my gun? I'd be weak. You'd report me to the police. I'd get a life sentence… or worse. To me, that's the same as dying."

Eva stepped forward, trying to reason with him. "You said you'd kill one of us first. So it was self-defense."

Doctor John nodded. "You're right. You rebelled with good reason. And I am taking appropriate action to protect myself."

His eyes darkened. "Does that upset you? A serial killer's life is worth less than a growing teenager's. A king's life… a pigeon's life… It's all the same." He waved them off. "Go upstairs."

Frank collapsed to his knees, begging for mercy. "Please, I'll do whatever you want—just don't kill Steve. Let him live!"

Doctor John remained silent.

"You're seven against one," he finally said. "You don't understand—I have to protect myself." He exhaled sharply. "Like I said, the rules need to be strict for the game to continue."

One by one, Jason, Richard, Gary, Eva, and Frank followed his orders, stepping into the upstairs dorm.

Michael hesitated before stepping inside last.

Doctor John escorted Steve to the auditorium.

Inside the locked room, Jason turned on Michael immediately. His fists flew, striking Michael hard.

"You did this!" he screamed. "You sided with him! You let the plan fail!"

Michael couldn't respond. The world was silent to him, and Jason's rage only grew.

Richard intervened, shoving Jason back. His eyes narrowed as he looked at Michael. "You can't hear, can you?"

Michael remained silent.

"Why didn't you say anything?" Richard asked, frustration bleeding into his voice.

Michael's mind was elsewhere, replaying Doctor John's words about the river where the lion waits.

In the auditorium, Doctor John and Steve faced each other, the gun between them.

Steve was motionless, his face unreadable. Doctor John hesitated for just a moment—then pulled the trigger.

A single shot rang out.

In the dorm upstairs, Jason, Richard, Gary, Eva, and Frank stiffened after hearing the voice of gunshot. Eva collapsed in tears. Frank sank to the floor.

Gary's eyes gleamed. Richard clenched his fists, his face twisting in anguish. Michael deaf to the sound simply stared unaware of what had just happened.

***

Finally, David and the hiker girl arrived at the school's gates.

David turned to her with a soft smile, "Welcome to the Jasper High."

Chapter 6

Turning the Tables?

David and Hiker Girl finally reached the school gates. He turned to her with a resigned expression.

"My reputation with the school is a bit... iffy. I had a little trouble with the teachers," David admitted.

The girl asked. "So, what do you want me to do?"

"I'll sneak into the school. You press the bell alone—you'll just be seeking shelter."

The girl hesitated. "I'm not good at that kind of thing."

David sighed. "Then let's find out what's going on first and decide."

She nodded in acknowledgment. They entered the school through the hall, and David led her to the boys' dorm, straight to his room. Later, she headed toward the bathroom for a shower, leaving David alone with his thoughts.

Sitting at his desk, he opened his laptop and checked the CCTV hack he had set up earlier. He scanned the footage. The upstairs room in teachers' dorm, where everyone was sitting, was too dark to see clearly. In the clinic, he saw Doctor John drinking water.

David whispered to himself, "Where has everyone gone?"

Despite his best efforts to stay focused, his thoughts kept drifting. His gaze lingered on the bathroom door for a moment before he shook his head and returned to his screen.

Meanwhile, Eva, feeling trapped and desperate, pushed against the locked door, trying and failing to escape.

At the same time, in the cafeteria, David and Hiker Girl argued over a plate of spicy eggs she had cooked.

"It's spicy!" David coughed.

"I told you it was spicy." She smirked.

"How much pepper paste did you use?"

"It has to be spicy to taste good," she defended.

David groaned. "My mouth is on fire. I'm a flamethrower!"

Hearing the commotion, Doctor John started heading over. Just as he neared, David and Girl quickly ducked under a table. Doctor John glanced down at the cafeteria from the first floor, then, seemingly uninterested, turned back toward the clinic.

The girl whispered, "Teacher..."

David shook his head. "He's not a teacher. He's Survivor No. 1."

A troubled expression crossed his face as he glanced around. Something felt off. Without a word, he peeled a cute band aid from his cheek and stuck it under the kitchen food table.

Eva sat near the locked door, her arms wrapped around herself. Richard approached her.

"You must think I'm stupid, right?" she muttered. "I tried to kill myself, but now, when we could really die, I throw up. You think I'm dumb."

Richard shook his head. "No, you're not stupid."

She looked up at him, her eyes glistening. "Richard?"

"Yes?"

Her voice trembled. "What do we do now? What should we do?"

Richard had no easy answers. He remained silent. It was a painful moment for both of them—a kind of defeat that settled deep into their bones.

Elsewhere, in the early morning hours, Jason tossed and turned in his assigned room at the teachers' dorm, once again haunted by nightmares of his mother.

In his dream, he was a young child, cold and shivering, pounding helplessly on his mother's apartment door, crying out for her. The memory was raw, vivid. It fueled his anxiety, leaving him restless even in sleep.

Jason jolted awake, breathing heavily. He got up and made his way toward the entrance door of the teachers' dorm, trying to open it—but failed. Suddenly, Doctor John appeared.

"I want to see you," Doctor John said.

Jason frowned. "Why?"

"I want to ask a favor."

Doctor John led Jason out of the lockdown. Soon, they entered Michael's room.

"I need you to find a battery for Michael's hearing aid," Doctor John instructed in his usual cold tone.

Jason frowned, confused. "Why does he need that?"

Doctor John's expression remained unreadable. "Without it, Michael is at a disadvantage." Jason was still trying to make sense of it all. "What do you mean by 'disadvantaged'?"

He looked around the room and eventually found the hearing aid battery. Doctor John looked at Jason and asked, "Who do you think sent the letter? Neither you nor I have evidence—just a hunch. What do you think happens next if we continue? Shock… Anger… Helplessness… What comes after that?"

Jason shook his head.

Doctor John leaned in slightly, "betrayal."

Jason clenched his jaw. "Are you trying to provoke me?"

Doctor John smirked. "Survival is our basic instinct. Actions taken to survive are all justified."

As they exited Michael's room, Jason asked, "Let's say someone confesses. How do we know they really sent the letters?"

Doctor John's reply was chilling. "We don't need evidence. A confession is all we need. It's the same as five of you accusing one person of being the sender. We don't need evidence for that either. There are two kinds of betrayal: One person betrays five of you, or five people betray one. If Michael doesn't hear this, then it's unfair."

Doctor John tilted his head slightly, emphasizing the gravity of his statement. "That's why I need Michael to hear. I'm playing fair, Jason. It's all about trust."

Meanwhile, in the locked teachers' dorm hall, Michael sat with Gary, Eva, Richard, and Frank. He shared a rare moment of clarity.

"I really had a counseling session about my childhood and animal documentaries," Michael admitted. "He didn't even ask about the letters. You don't talk at first, but you end up talking."

Richard sighed. "Doctor John is an expert at making people talk."

Frank glanced at Michael. "He didn't ask about the letters? So… is he really waiting for one of us to confess?"

Gary looked around suspiciously. "Who was it? Who sent them? It must be one of us... who was it? Raise your hand. We'll keep it a secret. Let's close our eyes."

Eva scoffed. "Then who will be able to see? We should find out who sent the letter first. That way, we can defend ourselves—"

Richard interrupted her. "Let's be curious about who sent the letter, knowing about the sender won't change anything. Let's say we do find out—do you think we can keep it a secret until the end?"

A heavy silence settled over the group.

Richard continued, "I'm angry at the person who sent the letters too. But that's not a reason for them to die. We can't let another death happen. So don't tell anyone who sent the letter. Not to us. Not to him. That's the only way we win.

Doctor John said it himself—the only evidence he has is a confession. If we trust each other, we can all survive this."

At that moment, Jason entered the dorm.

Frank eyed him warily. "Where did you go?"

Jason hesitated. "The doctor… we went to the boys' dorm."

Jason handed Michael the battery for his hearing aid.

Richard inquired. "What were you talking about? Did he say anything to you?"

Jason stayed silent. No reply.

At the cafeteria, Frank, Gary, and Michael were preparing breakfast plates, while Eva sat to Doctor John's left, and Richard and Jason sat in front of him.

Doctor John casually remarked on the events of the previous day. "Yesterday was a terrible day," he mused, his tone almost as indifferent as if he were commenting on the weather. "I hope that doesn't happen again."

Richard shot back sharply, his voice laced with anger. "You speak as though Steve's death was our fault."

Doctor John shrugged, as if the topic had little significance to him. "Let's say that I killed Steve. Who killed Tom? I overheard you talking while I had a fever. You killed someone too, right? Was it just a coincidence? Maybe the deceased student was too sensitive… but death is death, and murder is murder," he said coldly.

"I killed Steve because the situation forced me to. You made Tom take his own life, didn't you? So don't feel upset about this situation. We all deserve punishment."

Frank, frying eggs, glanced down at David's band aid, still lying on the table. It was a small detail, but it caught his attention. Michael whispered in Frank's ear, "What? What's wrong?"

At the same time, David was seated at his laptop, eyes fixed on the footage of the cafeteria. Hiker Girl slept on the bed nearby. David muttered to himself, "They all appear now, that it's time for breakfast." He was watching, as always, trying to maintain control, but something had escaped his notice. The students were eating, yes, but under the watchful eye of a gun.

Hiker Girl woke up, David quickly closed his laptop. Girl groggily asked, "What were you watching, something racy?"

David quickly responded, "I'm not a child."

Eva sat handcuffed to the cold metal table, unease creeping into her bones. Doctor John attempted to make small talk. "So, Eva, what do your parents do?" he asked.

"Why?" she replied, clearly uncomfortable.

"It's just chit-chat over a meal, If you don't want to talk about it, how about the weather? It's getting cold in the afternoon," Doctor John said.

Frank leaned over and subtly showed Richard the band aid, pressing it into his palm under the table. It was a quiet signal, a reminder that David might be watching.

Meanwhile, David, in his room, showed Hiker Girl a box and said, "I don't show this to anyone. It's called David's Times." He showed her a photo, "Look at this it was a bungee jump from my school." He pulled out a cap. "I bought this on the last school trip."

At the same moment, Richard and Jason were washing dishes. Doctor John continued to scan Eva's behavior. Eva stared back at him. "What?" she asked.

Richard, in a quiet gesture of defiance, started writing "SOS" on a piece of bread, hoping David would see it when he came for breakfast.

Jason, noticing Richard, asked, "What are you doing?"

Doctor John heard the noise and walked over to them. "Go against the wall," he ordered. As they stood straight, he examined them, then turned around and sat back down.

Later, Doctor John escorted them to the teacher's dorm entrance. "Who should I counsel now?" he asked, looking at them. "Jason, you stay here. The rest of you, go inside."

Doctor John locked the door behind them, taking Jason to the clinic.

In the teacher's dorm hall, Frank told Gary, Eva, Michael, and Richard, "I think David is back." He showed them David's band aid. Richard's eyes widened slightly as he understood the significance of the gesture. "This could be a turning point," he said. "Doctor John doesn't know about David."

Eva said, "But David doesn't know who Doctor John really is."

Richard replied, "We need to inform him. If David meets Doctor John without notice, he'll become another hostage."

Frank asked, "How do we let him know?"

Meantime, David, oblivious to the growing danger, was busy showing Hiker Girl his best Elmo impression—a bizarre distraction in the midst of this tense situation.

At the clinic, Doctor John had selected Jason for a counseling session, likely trying to exploit the boy's weaknesses further.

"Jason," Doctor John began, "You had a dream?"

Jason, his voice shaking, spoke. "I keep having nightmares… about my mom. About the punishments she used to give me." He stared at his hands, almost as if trying to make sense of his own words.

Doctor John asked, "Do you have that dream often?"

Jason nodded. "Yes, before exams, when I'm stressed."

***

David strolled into the cafeteria to grab breakfast then took it back to his room.

Later, in his room, David froze as His eyes fell on a plate of toast. He noticed something strange—SOS spelled out in jam on the surface of the bread. Hiker Girl, blissfully unaware, bit into the toast and chewed it without a second thought.

"You enjoy your breakfast?" David asked her. "I'll be back soon."

"Where are you going?" Hiker Girl asked.

"To get more food," David replied.

***

Back in the clinic, Jason continued to spill his secrets, though his words were inconsistent, as though he was second-guessing himself.

Doctor John scribbled on his notepad. "Jason, you refused to eat... you were thrown out of the house in your underwear?"

Jason replied, "I was wrong for doing that. My mother cooked for me, and I refused to eat. Of course, she was mad. I deserved the punishment. But you know, she wasn't always like that."

Doctor John's pen scratched across the paper as he made a note. "Jason, you said before that your mom usually forgave you when you stole a game console from your friend's house."

Jason replied, "My mom said kids do that... My mom never gave me fast food. She only gave me the best food, the best clothes. She washed all my clothes by hand, too. She prayed every night for my sins," Jason continued.

Doctor John asked, "Your mom went through all of your sins?"

Jason's voice wavered. "Why are you doing this? You're trying to make my mom look weird. You don't know her."

Doctor John replied, "Okay, I admit, your mom is perfect. So, you miss her, don't you? Is that why you see her in your dreams?"

Jason remained silent for a moment.

Doctor John pressed, "I don't mind, anyway. You didn't ask me to counsel you about your mom. Did you?"

Jason looked confused. "When did I ask you to be counseled?"

Doctor John leaned forward. "You looked at me."

Jason's expression hardened, "No way!"

Doctor John smiled faintly. "Tell me what you really want to say. Did I see wrong? I thought you wanted to tell me something."

Jason remained silent.

Doctor John leaned back in his chair. "I'm not a magician, Jason. I'm a therapist. I don't know anything until you tell me. Maybe I was wrong. Should we end the session here?"

Jason's eyes shifted uneasily. "What's wrong with me? What's bad about me?"

"You're not bad," Doctor John replied, his tone cold. "You're just weak. If people knew how weak you are, no one would hate you."

Jason's discomfort was evident, but he quickly lied, "I sent the letter. They pretend to be saints as though they didn't do anything wrong—Richard, Steve, Eva, I wanted to let them know what they did, so I sent the letters… Don't you believe me?"

Doctor John didn't buy it, but he let it slide. "I do believe you. I don't have any reason not to. So tell me—who committed the worst sin? Is it Steve, Eva, Michael, Richard, Gary, or Frank? If you hate them that much, you should be able to pinpoint someone. Who has the worst sin?"

Jason, his voice growing stronger, replied, "We never discussed that. You only told me to confess."

Doctor John pressed, "You have to be able to say it if you're not lying."

In the teacher's dorm hall, Richard was telling Eva, Michael, Gary, and Frank, "We have no other choice. We need to leave a memo for David at lunchtime."

Meanwhile, David saw the message and instantly understood its meaning. Hooking up his laptop to a series of wires leading to the clinic door, he set his plan in motion. Inside, Jason had already made his choice—the person he believed bore the worst sin.

Doctor John studied him carefully. "Let me check once more... the person you believe committed the worst sin—"

Before he could finish, a loud crash echoed outside. David had thrown a potted plant against the clinic wall. Doctor John immediately grabbed his gun and rushed to the door, reaching for the handle. The moment his hand made contact, a jolt of electricity surged through him. His body convulsed, and he collapsed, the gun slipping from his grasp.

The lights flickered as Jason lunged for the weapon, but before he could not reach to it, David strode into the room, completely unfazed. He picked up the gun with ease and tossed the handcuff keys to Jason, smirking.

"You're free now."

Jason stared. "How do you—?"

David cut him off. "Who is that guy?"

Jason hesitated. "What do you think? A serial killer."

David stunned. "Where are the others?"

The two of them hurried to the teachers' dorm and freed Gary, Richard, Eva, Michael, and Frank. The moment they saw David, they tackled him in a joyous dogpile. Their shouts of his name filled the air, their relief palpable.

"I have a gun in my hand, be careful!" David warned, laughing.

Everyone quickly backed off. Richard shook his head. "You should've said that earlier! We almost died as soon as we got our lives back."

Later, Doctor John awoke, handcuffed to a clinic bed. His vision blurred as he took in the sight of David sitting casually next to him, gun in hand.

David asked. "Are you okay, Mr. Serial Killer?"

Doctor John blinked, confused. "Who... are you?"

David grinned. "I'll introduce myself later."

His smile faded as he turned to Richard. "Where are Liam and Steve?" The moment the words left his mouth, the energy in the room shifted. His voice softened. "Are they really dead? That doesn't make sense."

The thought of Steve's absence weighed heavily, but he couldn't process it.

David crouched next to Doctor John. "Did you really kill Steve? What's wrong with you? What does someone have to go through to end up like you?"

Doctor John's gaze was steady, almost amused. "You think I'm that different from you?" His voice was eerily calm.

"People always ask about a serial killer's childhood. They want to believe there's an explanation—an alcoholic, violent father, a mother with too many lovers. But the truth is, it's a lie to make them feel safe. Not every monster comes from trauma. Some just are."

David narrowed his eyes. "What the hell are you talking about?"

Doctor John smirked. "The monster inside you. Can you feel it?"

Doctor John looked at gaze the group, lingering on Jason. "I can see it in some of you. You don't want to admit it, but it's waking up."

Jason snapped. Without thinking, he kicked Doctor John in the face. The others startled, and just then, Amanda stepped inside, letting out a surprised gasp.

Richard turned. "Who is she?"

David waved toward her. "This is Hiker Girl."

She corrected him. "Amanda."

"Right," David said. "Amanda, meet the students—and the serial killer."

After locking Doctor John in the detention cell, Jason, Gary, and Frank raided the teachers' dorm for alcohol, chips, and snacks. When they returned, David, Richard, and Eva were waiting in the Cafeteria.

David smirked. "What's this? Stealing from the teachers? You all have gotten daring."

Gary shrugged. "It's fine. If anyone asks, we'll just say the murderer drank it all."

Jason grinned. "Yeah. No one cares if a killer steals."

The celebration started. Even those who rarely smiled were laughing. David, the lifesaver and the life of the party, led a champagne fight.

The boys stormed outside into the snow, reveling in their newfound freedom. Jason, however, watched from the girls' dorm hallway window, distant.

Downstairs, Amanda moved oddly. She approached Eva, who was lying on the floor, seemingly unconscious. Just as Amanda reached out to touch her face, Eva's eyes snapped open.

"What are you doing?" she asked, her voice sharp.

Amanda tilted her head. "You're very pretty, Eva Mendis. It would be better if only you had a prettier name."

Eva frowned and walked away.

Later, in the corridor, Jason stopped Eva. "Hey."

She rolled her eyes. "What is it, Plague?"

Jason smirked. "What did you do with Richard last night?"

Eva laughed. "Oh, Jason, what do I have to do for you to stop liking me?"

Jason took a step closer, his voice low. "I already stop liking you. It was twisted enough for a twisted boy like me to like you. That's over now."

Eva's amusement vanished. Real fear flickered in her eyes as she backed into the wall. But Jason froze.

"What are you talking about?" she asked.

Jason turned and walked away.

Back in the cafeteria, Michael, Frank, David, and Richard returned from playing in the snow. Eva rushed in, her face tense.

"Jason was acting strange," she told Richard.

His stomach twisted. "Where's the gun?" he asked David.

***

In the detention room, Doctor John wasn't surprised when the door creaked open to reveal Jason, gun trembling in his hands.

Doctor John smirked. "I was waiting for you."

Jason's voice was strained. "Then it'll be over soon."

Doctor John asked. "Then why do you look so sad?"

"Sad? Me?"

Doctor John chuckled. "Afraid of betraying your friends?"

"Betrayal" Jason let out a bitter laugh. "If betrayal means turning your back on trust, then I've never betrayed anyone. No one trusted me to begin with. Lying, stealing—soon, even murder—I'm guilty of every crime except that one. I'm innocent of betrayal, your honor."

Doctor John smirked. "Then why do you want to kill me? Because I might tell them that you confessed?"

Jason slammed his head against the wall. Richard and the others burst into the room.

"Jason, put the gun down!" Richard urged.

Jason screamed, "Don't tell me what to do!"

"It's over now! Why are you doing this?"

Doctor John cut in. "Afraid they'll hate you if I tell them the truth? You're used to being hated, aren't you?"

Jason's voice cracked. "That's right. I'm used to it. So used to it that I feel scared when people don't hate me. So I do things to make sure they do."

Jason's gaze landed on Eva. "But people hating me and me hating myself are different."

He pointed the gun at Doctor John. "You made me hate myself!"

David called his name. Jason snapped, "Call me what you normally do."

David smirked. "What? The Plague?"

Jason, trembling, turned the gun on David. But David merely reached into his pocket, pulling out a handful of bullets.

"You think I'm stupid?" David asked. "Would I leave a loaded gun with a bunch of drunks?"

Jason dropped the gun and fell to his knees, sobbing. No one spoke. As he turned to leave, Frank quietly followed to make sure he reached his room safely.

Meanwhile, in the detention center, Richard, Michael, Gary, David, and Eva remained with Doctor John. Richard asked, "What did you tell Jason?"

Doctor John replied, "I told you before, what I discuss in my sessions is confidential."

David scoffed. "We should've let Jason kill him."

Doctor John sneered. "I have a favor to ask. Can you uncuff me?"

David got shocked by Doctor John request. "We're about to hang you upside down, and you're asking us to remove your handcuffs?"

Doctor John leaned forward. "I have something very important to tell you… Steve is alive."

At first, no one believed him. But Richard, thinking there was no harm in taking a chance, agreed to remove the handcuffs.

Once freed, Doctor John revealed the location: the dressing room in the auditorium. Without hesitation, Richard and David with others raced there, desperation fueling their steps. When they reached the door, they hesitated only a moment before bursting inside.

There, struggling to free himself was Steve.

Richard and David pulled him into a tight embrace before carrying him out. Their cheers were contagious. Eva ran up, throwing her arms around Steve as the others celebrated his return.

While the others took Steve to the cafeteria, Michael stayed behind, sitting on the stairs, overwhelmed with joy, tears streaming down his face.

Later, as Steve calmly ate dinner, David watched him in disbelief. "Look at you. You almost died. Shouldn't you, I don't know, be crying or something?"

Steve blinked then pointed to his head. "I have a problem on the left side of my brain. The nerves that send emotions are thinner than most."

David frowned. "What does that mean?"

"I can't feel emotions easily."

Amanda, passing by, brought more food for Steve. He turned to her. "Do you have a cell phone? We need to call for help."

Amanda nodded. "Yeah, but it's out of battery."

"Spare battery?"

She shook her head. "I didn't bring one."

Steve took her phone anyway. "I can make it work."

David chuckled. "Cell phones don't work here. That's why they're not allowed."

Steve ignored him. "Where did the avalanche happen? Was it in front of the bridge? We need to get close to the temple. We'll have signal there for sure."

Steve was already making plans, thinking ahead. David watched him in awe. "It's a good thing I gave up early," he muttered, realizing what it meant. He had given up—on competing with Steve.

Outside her room in Girls' dorm, Eva leaned against the wall, staring at the night sky. Richard approached.

"I wonder if it's really over now," she said softly. "Good night. I'm going to go have a nightmare."

Richard handed her the unloaded gun. "It doesn't have bullets, but you'll feel safe."

In the detention room, Doctor John removed the sling from his left arm. He winced as he tried to move it but found the pain bearable. He flexed his fingers—his hand was healing. He wouldn't need the sling anymore.

That night, David led Amanda to the girls' dorm. As they walked, he smirked. "Why do you like Eva?"

Amanda shrugged. "She's pretty."

David laughed. "You know, you're beautiful too."

Amanda rolled her eyes, but before she could respond, David stole a quick kiss. He instantly backed away, bracing himself for a hit. But Amanda only said, "I don't hit young boys for doing something wrong."

Taking that as permission, David leaned in again.

This time, he was met with a sharp slap.

Amanda smirked. "If you do the same thing twice, I'll hit you."

***

The next morning, Jason shuffled into the cafeteria, his movements hesitant, like a scared puppy. He was met with warm smiles and friendly greetings, as though the chaos of the previous night had been nothing more than a drunken misunderstanding.

David nudged Richard. "Look, its Jason."

Richard turned to him. "Is your head okay?"

Jason groaned. "It's killing me. I'm hearing bells in my head."

Richard handed him a cup of coffee. "Drink this."

Jason, visibly relieved, grinned and melted back into the group, grateful for a second chance.

Meanwhile, Steve, already on his feet, had managed to fix charged the battery of Amanda's cell phone. But they still needed to find a spot with a signal.

Later, Gary, Eva, Amanda, David, Frank, Michael, and Jason stood in front of Steve and Richard. As the two prepared to leave, Richard reassured them, "We'll be back before dark."

Frank waved. "See you soon."

Everyone watched as they disappeared into the snowy landscape.

Meanwhile, Amanda sat in her room, rummaging through her bag. She pulled out a Swiss Army knife, its metallic gleam catching the light, and then fished out the gun that Eva had hidden in her bed.

David made his way to the detention room where Doctor John sat quietly. David arrived with a smirk. "Good morning! Want to hear some good news? Two boys just left. Soon, you'll be off to prison. How do you feel about serving a life sentence?"

Doctor John, unruffled, simply shrugged. "I've lived twice as long as you. Life is full of surprises. You never know what waits for you at the end of the alley."

David grinned. "Wait... I can see it! Police cars at the end of the alley, and—oh, is that a prison I see?"

David laughed at his own joke before turning serious. "So what's your plan? Are you to fake insanity in court? You're an expert in that field, right? Drool a little, pretend to be crazy, and get sent to a mental institution instead?"

Doctor John didn't flinch. "I won't lie about it. I don't feel shame for what I've done. It's not pride, but I do feel a sense of responsibility. Murder is a difficult process. You don't do it without a sense of duty. So why should I lie?"

***

Steve and Richard were battling the cold on a snowy mountain road, trying to get a signal to call the police. Despite their best efforts, the line dropped just as the operator asked for a description of Doctor John. Frustrated, Steve handed the phone to Richard, who tried his best to give the details.

***

Back at the school, Amanda walked alone through the hallways, still carrying the gun. Eva, realizing it was missing, felt her heart sink. She knew what had happened.

***

The phone call finally went through After Richard finished speaking with the police something in the call log caught his eye. One call.

Made on the same day Doctor John arrived at the school from the Jasper High landline. The realization hit him like a freight train.

"Amanda," he whispered. The name of the woman—the one he had spoken to about Doctor John's accident.

***

At that very moment, Amanda confronted David in the detention room. Her expression was cold, but something dangerous lurked beneath the surface.

"Give me the bullets," she demanded.

David refused. She struck, slashing his hand with brutal precision. Blood splattered across the wall as David recoiled, his eyes wide with disbelief. Amanda didn't hesitate. She unlocked the detention cell, turning to Doctor John with a twisted sense of purpose.

"Teacher," she said.

Chapter 7

The Anatomy of a Monster

Doctor John stepped out of the detention room and introduced the real Amanda to David.

"This woman, Amanda... She was my first patient," he began.

"She was sexually abused since childhood, and it turned her into a mindless being. She shut herself off from the world like a hermit crab in its shell. She has a cycle of repression, escape, and obsession with a particular person. Just as a baby chick freshly hatched attaches itself to the first being it sees—she became my stalker. She is my escape, but also a double-edged sword. She is my weapon."

Meanwhile, Eva found Frank in the school's laundry room. "Where is that woman?" Eva asked.

"Who?" Frank replied.

"Amanda. She said she didn't have a spare battery, but look what I found in her bag." Eva held up Amanda's cell phone battery.

"I'm sure she stole the gun Richard gave me. I'm telling you, that woman is strange."

Back in the detention area, Doctor John examined David's injured hand. "The nerves are fine. You just need to control the bleeding. You may have a scar, but you should be relieved."

Doctor John showed David his own hand scar. "I was in surgery for three hours because of that blade."

Amanda murmured, "I'm sorry."

Eva and Frank approached the detention center. Just as David called out, "Don't come in!" it was too late. As they stepped inside, Amanda aimed the gun at them.

Meanwhile, in the dark cafeteria, Gary saw a half-blue-faced child counting, "One, two… three..." playing hide-and-seek.

Back in the detention area, Doctor John locked David, Eva, and Frank inside the detention room. Soon after, Amanda reset Doctor John's dislocated shoulder and immediately apologized for causing him pain. David, royally pissed, glared at them from the detention cell while Frank tended to his injured hand.

Later, Doctor John walked toward the clinic. Michael saw him from afar, stunned, and quickly hid as Doctor John passed by. Once the coast was clear, Michael hurried to his room, packed his belongings into a small bag, and went into hiding.

***

Realizing Amanda was at the school, Richard began trekking through the snow to return. Steve asked, "Why are you in such a hurry? If Amanda helps Doctor John escape, they won't get far in this weather."

Richard responded, "Amanda could try to take hostages again."

"She can't do that all by herself," Steve said.

"The gun," Richard stressed.

"You have the gun, right?" Steve questioned.

Richard's guilty expression confirmed he didn't.

Tensions escalated as Steve demanded, "Why would you give Eva a gun without bullets? I don't get you and Eva."

Richard snapped, "Not everyone is like you! Do you think we all think with our heads and not our hearts?"

Steve was genuinely surprised by Richard's outburst, unaware that Richard was about to explode. "What's wrong with you?" Steve asked.

"You're treating me like a fool!" Richard yelled.

Steve slowly started to walk away. "When it comes to Eva, your head seems to freeze."

The argument ended when Richard lunged at Steve from behind, tackling him to the ground. A fight broke out, with both landing punches. Then, in the heat of the struggle, Richard accidentally shoved Steve away, sending him tumbling down the hillside.

Doctor John returned to the detention room, unlocking the cell and gesturing for Eva and Frank to step out. Behind the glass panel of the door, David remained inside.

"Aren't you running away?" David asked, watching him carefully.

Doctor John smirked. "I have something to do."

David peered. "If you wanted to kill us, you would've done it by now. You're not even curious about who sent the letters. What do you really want?"

Doctor John leaned against the door. "David, I don't think you were there when we were having lunch the other day. The news was on the radio—about me, a serial killer, a monster." He let the words hang in the air, savoring them. "Richard, Frank, Michael, Eva, Jason and Steve never realized that the serial killer they were talking about was sitting right there with them."

David stiffened.

"I remember what Steve said — are monsters like him born or made? That question has haunted me all my life. And now, I'm running an experiment. You, the most gifted students in the country, will help me find the answer." Doctor John's eyes gleamed with sick excitement. "If I can push you into becoming monsters, then monsters are made. But if you resist… then I was born this way." He chuckled. "Isn't that fascinating? The incubation has begun, and soon, we'll see what hatches from the shell."

***

Richard crouched beside Steve, who lay at the bottom of the cliff, clutching his broken leg.

"What's wrong?" Richard called down.

Steve groaned, trying and failing to move. "I think I broke my leg." His breath came in pained gasps as he tried to drag himself toward the rock wall.

Richard clenched his hands into fists. He knew Steve wasn't going to be able to climb out on his own. Panic surged in his chest.

Steve curled into himself, bracing against the bitter cold, his body already resigning to its fate.

***

In the school cafeteria, Doctor John sat across from Eva, gun in hand. He turned to Frank. "You have thirty minutes to bring someone here. You can run—they've probably already reported to the police. Stay hidden for a day, you might just make it out free… you can leave Eva behind to save yourself. I don't care either way."

Doctor John's smile widened. "As I said, I want to see you turn into monsters. Your 30 minutes start now."

Frank hesitated, "who?"

Doctor John smirked. "Jason."

"Why Jason? Why not Michael or Gary?" Frank asked.

"Just before they gave me the electric shock," Doctor John said, "Jason confessed to sending the letters."

Eva's jaw tightened. "Jason, jerk?"

Doctor John shrugged. "I have my doubts about his confessions, but without proof, I have to believe him." He glanced at his watch. "Your time has already started."

Frank swallowed, knowing the truth—Jason hadn't sent the letters. But he had no choice. Instead of looking for Jason right away, he rushed to his room, grabbed Tom's diary, and braced himself for what was coming.

In the school's detention area, Amanda sat beside David, folding a delicate paper flower. She held it up to him.

"Isn't it pretty?"

David barely glanced at it. "I'm not really in a position to admire artwork right now."

Amanda pouted. "Sorry. Does it hurt a lot?"

"I could die," David muttered.

Amanda tilted her head. "You should've given me the bullets when I asked."

David stiffened. "He's going to kill us."

Amanda smiled softly. "Teacher won't do that. You and Eva are good kids."

David's voice turned sharp. "And if he does?"

Amanda blinked. Then, in an eerily calm voice, she said, "Then you're not good kids."

Meanwhile, Doctor John sipped his tea, sitting across from Eva in the cafeteria.

"Are you enjoying this?" Eva asked bitterly.

Doctor John exhaled in satisfaction. "Yes. I'm excited to see which monster hatches first."

Eva glared at him. "Even if someone does snap, they won't be like you. You're twisted—evil, one of a kind."

Doctor John's smile widened. "No living creature is born complete. They grow. Do you know who I'm looking forward to the most?" Eva didn't respond.

"Richard."

She stiffened. "Richard? No. He'd die before becoming a monster."

Doctor John chuckled, "because his mother died saving him?"

Eva's breath caught.

"I had read Richard's file—a pre-check before the consultation. She saved her son and was hit by a car, but what about the boy who lived?"

Doctor John continued. For a five-year-old, losing his mother would feel like losing the world. His scar would never fully heal. He's spent his life trying to be the son his mother would be proud of. But the tighter the elastic is stretched, the harder it snaps when it breaks." His voice turned gleeful.

"When Richard's monster awakens, it'll be bigger than all of ours combined."

"Ridiculous," Eva spat.

Doctor John just smirked. Amanda walked in with Gary.

***

At the wreckage of the police car, Richard rifled through the debris, his fingers numb from the cold. He found a length of rope—and an empty gun. He paused, giving a brief, respectful nod to the frozen officers before sprinting back toward Steve.

Steve's shivering had worsened his body on the brink of shutting down. But when Richard's rope landed beside him, a spark of hope reignited in his eyes.

With trembling hands, Steve secured the rope around himself, ready for one last attempt at survival.

Richard gritted his teeth and began pulling, one agonizing tug at a time.

***

At the school theater, Frank found Jason watching a movie.

Jason asked, "Have you seen this movie? It's very good."

"David wants to see you," Frank said.

Jason frowned. "Why?"

"He wants to talk about what to do when the police arrive."

Jason hesitated then shrugged, "alright."

As they walked through the hall, Jason glanced around. "Aren't Richard and Steve back yet?"

Frank kept walking. "Not yet."

"They should've been back by now," Jason muttered.

Frank didn't reply.

When they reached the restroom, Jason paused. "I need to pee."

Frank waited by the sink, washing his hands.

Jason spoke up again. "Isn't there a reward for catching a serial killer? Do we get a medal? Maybe bonus points for university?"

Frank's expression darkened.

Jason noticed. "You look different. What's wrong?"

Frank grabbed a wooden stick from the cleaning supplies near the door. He walked toward Jason.

Jason turned, confused. "Frank?"

Frank swung the stick.

Jason dodged. The stick smashed into the mirror, glass shards scattering across the sink.

Jason bolted. Frank chased him. The hunt had begun.

Jason sprinted into an empty classroom, breathing hard. Frank followed, searching between the desks.

"Where are you, Jason?" Frank taunted. "The doctor wants to see you. I heard what you told him—that you sent the letters, really? You surprised me."

Jason crouched behind a desk, heart pounding.

When Frank found him, Jason turned the tables—tackling him to the floor.

"You psycho" Jason roared, fists crashing into Frank's face. "You dare fool me?"

Frank gasped, blood pouring from his nose. He struggled to reach the stick, but Jason pinned him down.

"You all talked about how to survive!" Jason screamed. "And when I do it, I'm the villain?"

Frank's vision blurred from the punches. Jason's voice rang in his ears, but his body was shutting down.

Jason stood up, breathing heavily. "Don't criticize me. You'd let someone else die in your place too."

Frank, bloodied and dazed, whispered, "No… I wouldn't…"

Jason turned to leave. Frank's fingers closed around the stick. With a sickening crunch, he swung.

Jason crumpled to the floor. But Frank wasn't done. He hit him again... and again... and again. "Not me! I wouldn't! I'm not you!"

The words came between frantic, violent swings, his voice trembling with denial. Jason's groans weakened. The air in the room grew thick. And Frank... kept swinging.

Back at the school's cafeteria, Gary, Eva, and Doctor John were sitting while Amanda stood next to them. Gary mentioned that the child with the half-blue face, whom he called the "Monster in the Corner," had begun counting, searching for him.

Doctor John asked, "Why do you think the Monster in the Corner started counting?"

"To put pressure on me," Gary replied.

"Why he put Pressure on you?" Doctor John probed.

"To remember... to find him," Gary clarified.

Doctor John leaned in slightly. "Do you want to know who the Monster in the Corner is?"

As soon as Gary answered, "Yes," Doctor John took out his pen and tapped it against the table. Almost instantly, Gary fell asleep.

Eva watched the entire exchange with suspicion.

***

On the mountain, Richard's hands were raw, the rope cutting into his skin as he pulled Steve higher. Jason's words echoed in his mind: "Steve is a born genius that Richard can never beat. You want to kill him, right?" The words rang in his ears like an incessant drumbeat, and for a moment, his grip faltered.

Steve slipped downward, and Richard's heart skipped a beat. He could let go. He could let Steve fall, just as Jason had suggested. But then, with a roar, Richard tightened his grip, his fingers digging into the rope as though it was the only thing keeping him alive.

Richard pulled again, blood seeping from his hands, but he wouldn't stop. He refused to let Steve die. Finally, exhausted and bloodied, Richard managed to haul Steve to safety. When Steve was on solid ground, Richard collapsed, his legs too weak to hold him any longer.

"Are you alright, Richard?" Steve asked, his voice shaky.

Richard nodded. "Yes."

Steve, though cold and pale, looked at Richard with a mixture of disbelief and gratitude. "I thought you wouldn't come," he admitted.

***

In the school classroom, Frank, his hands trembling with rage, struck Jason repeatedly until the stick splintered in his grasp. For a moment, he stood frozen, staring at the blood on his hands. His reflection in the broken mirror showed a monster he could no longer ignore.

With a defeated slump, Frank dropped to the floor, curling into a fetal position.

Meanwhile, Dr. John continued his hypnotic session. Gary sat in the chair, his mind drifting through the murky fog of his memories.

"Where are you right now?" Dr. John asked.

"At home," Gary replied.

"Look around. Who is there?"

"Mom."

"What is she doing?"

"Cooking pancakes."

Dr. John's voice remained calm, methodical. "Now, we are going to find the Monster in the Corner. Where should we begin?"

"In the closet."

Dr. John guided him gently, coaxing him toward the closet door where the monster lurked, waiting to be freed. "Open the door, Gary."

Gary hesitated, trapped in fear.

Finally, after what seemed like an eternity, Gary broke free from the trance. His eyes snapped open, a cold clarity settling in. "I want to stop."

Eva, watching from the sidelines, felt a chill creep over her. Dr. John's actions triggered something deep within her own memories.

"You've done this to me before! Just before I tried to commit suicide!" she yelled. "Did you hypnotize me too?"

Dr. John shrugged nonchalantly. "You reacted well to hypnosis. Gary didn't."

Eva's anger flared, her heart pounding. "Did you tell me to slit my wrists?"

Dr. John remained impassive. "It was part of the therapy."

Eva's fury boiled over. "When did I ever ask you to hypnotize me? What did you find out about me?"

"Why you hate yourself. Your love and respect toward your mother. And about your mom's affair"

Enraged, Eva hurled a cup at him. In an instant, Amanda leaped across the table, gripping Eva's hair and smashing her face into the surface.

Dr. John, as if calling off a wild animal, commanded, "Enough. Stop."

Amanda reluctantly obeyed and stood next to him.

Dr. John looked at Eva. "You wanted to die after discovering your mother's affair, but that was nothing more than a child's whining. The most effective treatment for a delicate flower like you was to make you realize what death truly felt like. And it worked—you don't talk about suicide anymore."

At that moment, Frank dragged Jason into the cafeteria. Frank opened his mouth to speak, but Dr. John held up a hand. "Wait."

Eva stared at him as he continued. "Do you still want to slit your wrists?"

Then, Dr. John aimed a gun at her head. "If you still want death, I'll make it happen for you."

***

Richard felt something was off as he helped Steve back toward the school.

***

In the cafeteria, Dr. John stood calmly, the gun still pointed at Eva's head. "You have until the count of three to decide whether you want to live or die," he said. "One... two..."

Eva's heart raced. Tears streamed down her face. She had no choice but to beg, her voice breaking with fear. "I want to live. I want to live with my mom. Please, save me."

For a second, Dr. John's expression softened, and the gun lowered. "End of therapy," he said with a smile.

But before Eva could breathe a sigh of relief, Dr. John aimed the gun at her again. His face was cold. "It's a pity. Yesterday, when Jason confessed that he sent the letters. He pointed to you as having the worst sins."

Dr. John turned to Jason. "Tell us why you chose Eva. Perhaps you don't want to answer?"

Eva's eyes went to Jason, but his face was blank, emotionless. His voice was flat as he looked at Eva. "I hated you. I hated you when you were with Richard. I hated you after you broke up with Richard. I hated the way you ridiculed me. I wanted to kill you because you pitied me."

Dr. John sighed. "It's a shame you realized you wanted to live. Shall we finish the game now?"

Just as he prepared to pull the trigger, Frank stepped forward. "The game isn't over yet. Jason didn't send the letters. I did."

Dr. John asked. "Do you have evidence?"

Frank pulled out Tom's diary and handed it to Dr. John.

Eva looked at Frank, stunned. "Why?"

"I wrote them because someone died, and no one felt guilty. That made me mad. I wanted them to realize what they'd done to Tom."

Dr. John's smile returned. "Frank, speak on behalf of the dead. Tell me—who among us has committed the greatest sin regarding Tom's death?"

Frank hesitated, then answered, "I'll tell you when everyone is here."

Dr. John smirked. "Are you trying to buy time? I can't allow that."

Frank's voice was steady. "Then you pick. What if I name Steve or Richard? Three out of six are not here. You want me to pick? That's no fun."

Dr. John considered this. "What if Steve and Richard don't come back?"

"They will," Frank said. "If Amanda is right about the roads being closed due to snow, they can't stay out all night. They'll return before dark."

Just then, Gary collapsed from his chair. Dr. John ordered Amanda to take him to the clinic, handcuff him, and then bring David to the teachers' dorm.

Later, Dr. John led Eva, Jason, David, and Frank to the teachers' dorm and locked them inside. He looked at Frank. "Will you be alright?"

Frank asked. "What do you mean?"

"Do you think the others will harm you?" Dr. John questioned.

Frank glanced at the furious Jason and replied, "If someone attacks me, they better be prepared to kill me. Otherwise, I'll point them out as the one with the worst sin."

Dr. John smiled and locked the door behind him.

Inside the teachers' dorm, Frank, Eva, and Jason sat in tense silence. The air was thick with unease as Eva finally broke the stillness.

"Tell us, Frank, what you are going to do?" she asked.

Frank blinked, confused. "What?"

"You bought time, now what?" Eva pressed.

Frank sighed. "I don't have any other plans. I'll name someone once Steve and Richard return."

Eva scoffed, "the most sinful? Do you even know what that means?"

Frank leaned back, his voice calm but laced with something darker. "I dreamed of this situation—everyone listening to me, watching my every move, the moment I become the center of attention."

Eva shook her head. "You must be happy then. Your dream finally came true. Don't you feel guilty? You put us all in this mess."

Frank's expression hardened. "I heard you laughing with Richard about Tom's love letter. You said it yourself—none of us are pure, sinless victims. Every single one of you played a part in Tom's death. You should all repent... over and over again—until I am convinced."

Meanwhile, Richard and Steve stood at the edge of the school grounds, panting from their sprint. Richard held up an object for Steve to see—a gun.

"I found it next to the car," Richard said, handing it over.

Steve checked the chamber. "No bullets. It's empty."

They reached the main entrance. Richard swiped his card, but the door didn't budge.

"What's wrong?" Steve asked.

Richard scowled. "Security level changed. We can't open the door unless someone lets us in from inside."

Suddenly, Richard's gaze locked onto the statue of the school president. He stood still, as if remembering something crucial.

Inside the teachers' dorm, David turned to Frank. "What will you do?"

Frank sighed. "I wish I had a plan… but keeping a secret is exhausting. Maybe that's why I've grown tired before the rest of you. I just want this to be over."

David peered out the window and spotted Richard outside. "Richard is back. I can see him."

David moved to open the window, but Eva stopped him. "Don't! The alarm will go off."

Down below, Richard knelt in the snow and wrote two words: Secret Passage.

David scanned the room for something to mark the map. Jason, noticing a lipstick tube on the counter, tossed it to him. David quickly sketched the passage on the window.

At the same time, in Michael's room, Doctor John searched for him but found only a crudely drawn map of the same passage.

Richard crawled through the air ducts, whispering to Steve, "Stay here. I'll be back soon."

Michael, hidden in the rafters, watched silently, not alerting them to his presence.

In the cafeteria, Richard tried to sneak up on Amanda with a wooden stick, but she was faster. With one swift move, she disarmed him and knocked him to the ground.

Just when Richard was about to be dragged away, Steve's voice rang out. "Let him go!"

Steve, with a broken leg, held the empty gun steady, convincing Amanda it was loaded. Richard seized the moment to tie Amanda's hands.

Before they could leave to gather the others, Doctor John entered, holding a gun—a loaded one. He grabbed Richard by the arm, pointed the gun at his head, and smirked. "Where on earth have you been, Richard?"

Steve didn't lower his gun, still keeping it trained on Amanda, while Doctor John saw an opportunity to have some fun.

"Goodness, what should we do now?" Doctor John said with mock cheerfulness.

Meanwhile, Michael silently made his way to the boys' dorm, entered David's room, opened his laptop, and started watching the CCTV footage.

At the same time, Doctor John held a gun to Richard's head, while Steve kept his gun trained on Amanda's back.

Doctor John smirked. "We can't stay like this all night," he said, glancing at Steve. "You look like you're on the verge of collapsing. How about we both drop our guns on the count of three? If not, shall we both fire... on the count of three?"

Amanda froze, surprise flashing in her eyes as she realized what Doctor John was saying—he was essentially telling her that her life meant nothing to him.

Doctor John continued, his voice taunting, "It's simple. But Steve, have you ever killed anyone in your life?"

Steve's grip on the gun tightened. "Don't you think I can fire?" he shot back.

Doctor John's gaze was amused. "I don't know."

Steve hesitated. "I… I don't know emotions like guilt or conscience. I don't know about Richard, but I can fire."

Doctor John checked his watch. "One minute until 7 PM. The bell will ring seven times, on the last chime… I will pull the trigger."

Steve's resolve cracked. He glanced at Richard—he couldn't let him die. Slowly, he lowered the gun.

Doctor John smiled and traded Richard's life for Steve's gun. As Richard passed Amanda, he whispered, "What are you to him? His girlfriend, is follower or just an accessory? I wouldn't bet on the life of a woman I liked. You know he's using you."

A little later, Doctor John tried to help untie Amanda hands, but she shoved him away—a subtle yet telling rejection.

Richard dragged Steve to the teachers' dorm, and as they entered, everyone's faces fell at the sight of Doctor John trailing behind.

Doctor John locked them in the room. He looked at Frank and said, "If you're ready, we should finish the game now. But we're not quite ready on our side because of some unnecessary chatter. Sorry, give me 30 minutes—I'll be back in half an hour," he said casually.

Doctor John went to the cafeteria and wasted no time, immediately working to win Amanda back. He knew exactly how to manipulate her and used his hold on her to pull her back under his control.

Doctor John patted Amanda's head like a puppy. "Just wait a little longer. It will be over soon."

He handed her a loaded gun. "Take it."

"What about you?" Amanda asked.

"It's fine. You'll come running if I'm in danger," he said smugly.

Amanda nodded quietly as Doctor John left. She then turned to begin preparing the dining table. She took out fruits and cake from the fridge and found candles in one of the drawers. After setting the cake on the table, she carefully arranged the other items before heading to the girls' dorm.

Meanwhile, Michael, hidden in David's room, watched the events unfold through CCTV.

Inside the dorm, the group made a plan: hide in different corners, turn off all the lights, and arm themselves with blunt weapons.

Frank, however, was left out of the plan entirely.

Doctor John entered the darkened teachers' dorm, his eyes gleaming with excitement. "Fighting back until the very last moment... that makes it fun."

Doctor John methodically checked each room, a grin spreading across his face as he reveled in the twisted excitement of the game.

"I'll enjoy this too. Whose plan is this, I wonder?" he mused, his eyes gleaming with anticipation. "Of course, Richard masterminded it. Steve wouldn't be reckless enough to come up with something like this."

Doctor John paused, eyes narrowing as he made his next prediction. "Let me guess—Richard will be the first to attack. He's too proud to stay hidden for long."

Doctor John opened a door, revealing Eva and Steve, who had managed to hide themselves successfully. He moved on, continuing his little game, trying to outthink them at every turn.

"David will be second," he muttered under his breath. "But who will be third? Steve's injured, and Eva's a girl... It must be poor Jason."

But when Doctor John opened a door, his eyes fell on Frank—tied up, duct tape over his mouth.

Doctor John sneered. "Didn't I tell you not to trust your friends? You actually believed in them?"

Meanwhile, Amanda, now wearing a white dress like a bride, carried a gun and matches.

Amanda entered the cafeteria, her eyes immediately drawn to the wreckage. The table was overturned, cake and fruit scattered across the floor in a messy heap. Amidst the chaos, a laptop sat open.

Footage played of Doctor John in a detention cell—old footage, yet it felt live.

In a sudden rush of urgency, Amanda ran off to the detention room to save Doctor John.

Back in the hallway of the teachers' dorm, Frank walked ahead, the gun trained on him the entire time. Doctor John followed closely, a smirk playing at the corners of his lips.

"Can you find your 'bad' friends for me?" Doctor John taunted.

Frank didn't look back. "I don't need to. Wherever they hide, they can still hear my voice." He paused for a moment, his mind clearly turning over the thoughts that had plagued him. "I kept thinking about who was the worst, about who was most involved in Tom's death," he admitted, his tone darkening. "Jason, Gary, Richard, Eva, Michael, Steve... among them, the one most sinful of all... was Tom himself. Tom was the worst."

Everyone, hidden in their corners, seemed taken aback by Frank's shocking admission.

Meanwhile, Amanda reached the detention cell. She burst in expecting to find Doctor John—but Michael shoved her inside, locking the door behind her. She managed to grab his hearing aid just before the door slammed shut.

In the dorm, Doctor John sneered. "That's a disappointing answer…"

Frank interrupted. "No. The most sinful person is the one who replaced Tom. It's me."

The group emerged from their hiding spots, surrounding Doctor John.

Amanda, locked in the detention cell, fired her gun at the Plexiglass.

The boys heard the shot and immediately realized Doctor John's gun must have been the one without the bullets.

Richard screamed. "Doctor John's gun... is empty!"

They charged—but Doctor John was faster. He slipped away, dragging Frank with him, locking the others inside.

From outside the school, police sirens blared, and a loudspeaker crackled to life. A police officer's voice rang out: "You are surrounded! I repeat, you are surrounded!"

Chapter 8

The Monster's Last Laugh

Earlier that morning, at the police station, Detective Reynolds played a recorded call for the team. The voice on the tape was unmistakable: "This is Steve from Jasper High. There's a serial killer who calls himself Doctor John. He's in our school."

Detective Reynolds, who was in charge, turned to the others, explaining, "This call was made at 11 a.m. today. The owner of the cell phone is Amanda Kane... She's a patient of Doctor John."

One of the officers asked, "Is Amanda with Doctor John there?"

Detective Reynolds replied, his expression grim, "We're not sure about that yet."

The police wasted no time. They knew immediately that Doctor John, the notorious serial killer, was likely on the premises, along with his patient, Amanda.

Using a massive snowplow to clear the blocked roads, the police made their way to the school. But just as they reached the gates, a gunshot rang out through the cold, snowy air—the shot Amanda had fired at the plexiglass in the detention cell.

The police set up camp just outside the school gates. Detective Reynolds grabbed a megaphone, calling out, trying to make contact with Doctor John. "This area is surrounded. We heard the gunfire. What was that sound? Is anybody hurt?"

Meanwhile, Doctor John, holding Frank hostage, entered the broadcasting room. He peered through the window and used the school's PA system to respond. His calm voice crackled through the speakers, sending a chill through everyone listening.

"You all know me, so I'll skip the introductions. I'm with eight students right now, and they're all safe. Both my partner and I are armed. The gunfire you heard was just a warning. If you come any closer, it will be more than just a warning."

In the clinic, Gary was handcuffed to a hospital bed. In the teachers' dorm, Steve, struggling with his broken leg, shivered from the cold. Richard was taking care of him, while Jason, David, and Eva sat nearby, listening to the exchange between the police and Doctor John through the PA system and the loudspeakers outside.

Inside the detention cell, Amanda fought desperately to break the bulletproof glass, frustration building with every failed attempt. Michael, who had been watching from outside, couldn't help but mock her.

"It's useless. Even Mad David couldn't break out. What makes you think you stand a chance?"

Amanda, her anger flaring, pointed the gun at Michael through the plexiglass door. "Open the door," she demanded.

"There's no point in killing me," Michael replied coolly. "That door can only open from the outside."

The exchange outside continued as Doctor John outlined his demands to the police.

Detective Reynolds asked, "Doctor John, what do you want?"

Doctor John's voice remained calm. "I've been holding counseling sessions with the students. It's impossible to uncover deep-rooted problems in just a few sessions, but it has been... intriguing. What I want is to continue these sessions until the end. In the final stage, I would like to speak with their parents. Once I have finished consulting with them, I will return the students."

Detective Reynolds pressed, "You will set them free?"

Doctor John responded simply, "Yes."

The police scrambled to meet his conditions, organizing transportation for the parents while preparing SWAT teams, helicopters, and snipers stationed on the school rooftop.

Gary's parents arrived first. As they walked toward the police camp, Outside, Detective Reynolds coached the parents on what they should and shouldn't say to avoid arousing suspicion.

Detective Reynolds called out, "Doctor John, Gary's parents are here."

Using Frank as a human shield, Doctor John crossed the hallways, sniper lasers trained on them the entire time. He made his way to the clinic, where he unshackled Gary and led him to the broadcasting room.

Finally, Doctor John responded to Detective Reynolds, his voice tinged with amusement, "Apologies for the delay."

Gary's father stepped forward. "I'm Gary's father. I want to speak to my son first!"

Doctor John placed the PA system's microphone close to Gary. "It's me, Dad," Gary said hesitantly.

Gary's mother interrupted, her voice trembling. "It's me, Mom! Are you safe, my son?"

"Yes, Mom."

Detective Reynolds pushed again. "Doctor John, as you promised, please set Gary free."

Doctor John chuckled. "Of course. But first, I need to confirm if they are really his parents. They arrived earlier than expected—it bothers me. So, let's do a simple quiz. Don't be nervous. If you are his real parents, you'll answer easily."

Gary's mother hesitated. "A quiz?"

Doctor John's voice remained smooth. "Tell me, how do you make pancakes?"

Gary's mother stammered. "What? Pancakes?"

An officer beside her discreetly searched for a recipe on his phone. But Doctor John continued, his words unsettling.

"I was moved when Gary told me about this. He said his mother hugged him a lot when he was young. That she made up a story about a monster in the corner. I asked him, 'When were you happiest?' Do you know what he said? When his mother made pancakes for him. Even now, the smell of pancakes reminds him of her."

Doctor John's voice hardened. "So, tell me again—how do you make pancakes?"

Gary's mother, visibly shaken, recited the recipe she had just read.

Doctor John smirked. "Stop. You sound like you're reading from a cookbook."

Her mask cracked. "What's the point of all this?" she snapped.

Doctor John smiled. "You just proved you really are Gary's mother. I will return your son to you."

But Gary looked anything but relieved. His mind reeled, flashing back to childhood—a boy playing with a warm, gentle woman. But she wasn't his mother.

Meanwhile, in the teachers' dorm, Steve burned with fever from an infected leg. Richard, concerned, prepared an ice pack and reassured him, "Doctor John is keeping his word. Just hold on a little longer."

At the school's entrance, Gary turned to Doctor John. "How did you know? That the woman who made pancakes and talked about monsters wasn't my real mother?"

Doctor John paused. "I only just realized it now."

Gary's memories came flooding back—police bursting into a house, arresting the woman who had raised him. The woman who had once kidnapped him.

"Who was she?" Gary whispered. "Why did I think she was my mother?"

Doctor John's voice softened. "Memories work in strange ways, Gary. Sometimes the truth destroys people. Do you still want to know it?"

Gary hesitated, then shook his head and walked toward the police camp.

A sudden sniper shot rang out. Everyone flinched, but no one was hurt. Yet the tension skyrocketed. Doctor John lost his composure, his voice sharp with fury.

"I kept my promise. And this is what I get in return?" He stepped forward, arms spread wide. "Shoot me if you want. I'm right here! Want to know my location? Rear building, second floor, broadcasting room. Go ahead, aim for my heart!"

The police remained silent.

Doctor John's tone turned venomous. "But remember, my partner will kill the students. And that will be your fault."

Detective Reynolds clenched his jaw. "It was a mistake."

Doctor John snapped. "A mistake? Then should I make a mistake, too? Should we 'accidentally' fire as well?"

Detective Reynolds swallowed his pride. "I'm sorry. Please, calm down."

Inside the school;s detention room, Amanda clutched two bullets tightly, her mind racing. She muttered under her breath, "Doctor... rear building... second floor."

Then, she made her decision.

Outside, Detective Reynolds questioned Gary. "We've confirmed four students in the teachers' dorm. Do you know where Doctor John is keeping the others?"

"I don't know," Gary replied.

"Is Amanda guarding the students at gunpoint?"

"I don't know. I was in the clinic."

"What did Doctor John discuss in his sessions with you?"

Before Gary could answer, his mother cut in. "Stop it! He just got out! Can't you see he's still anxious?" She grabbed Gary's arm and pulled him away.

Meanwhile, in the detention center, Amanda worked desperately to dismantle a bullet. She wrapped the gunpowder in paper and stuffed it into the door's lock. With two matches in her hands, she struck one and stepped back.

Nothing happened.

Outside, the haunting strains of Mozart's Requiem echoed through the school's PA system, controlled by Doctor John.

Michael, though deaf, understood what Amanda was attempting. "What are you doing? Don't!" he pleaded. "You'll hurt yourself too!"

Amanda ignored him. She lit the second match.

This time, the explosion rocked the door. Flames burst out. The lock shattered.

Michael watched in horror as Amanda stepped out, unscathed. She handed him his hearing aid, and only then did he see the blood staining her clothes—a chilling reminder of the cost of her actions.

Amanda's back was drenched in blood, the blast having caught her just in time. She stumbled through the school's glass-enclosed bridge, sniper lasers tracking her every move. But she barely noticed. She had only one focus. Doctor John.

With unsteady steps, she made her way toward him. Blood dripped behind her, a silent witness to her resolve.

Finally, she reached him. Doctor John's expression twisted in shock as he saw her bloodied form.

Amanda whispered, "I'm sorry."

She handed him the gun and bullets—a final gesture of trust—before collapsing into his arms.

For the first time, Doctor John looked afraid. In trying to create the perfect monster, he had lost control of his creation.

Amanda's smile remained, even as blood trickled down her lips. She smeared her blood across Doctor John's cheek.

With a quiet, chilling smile—Amanda died in his arms. Doctor hugged Amanda and started to cry.

In the teachers' dorm, Steve convulsed violently from his worsening fever. David, panicked, screamed for the police to hurry, demanding they break through the doors and save them.

Outside, Eva's parents arrived. Detective Reynolds informed Doctor John, "Eva's parents are here."

Doctor John made his way to the teachers' dorm to retrieve Eva. Inside, Richard, Eva, Jason, and David stood on the other side of the door. Holding up two guns, Doctor John challenged them, "Which one is loaded, and which one isn't?"

Eva's eyes briefly met Richard's. He offered her a reassuring smile and patted her shoulder. "I'm relieved you get to go first," he said quietly. His words, though unexpected, provided some comfort.

As Doctor John led Eva toward the broadcasting room, Michael fumbled with his hearing aid, realizing it wasn't working.

At the broadcasting room, Eva sat at the table with the microphone. Doctor John addressed the waiting parents. "Sorry for the delay. You may speak to your daughter."

"Eva?" her mother called out.

"Mom!" Eva responded.

"Are you okay? Are you hurt?" her father asked.

"No," Eva reassured him.

"It's okay, everything will be fine," her father said.

"Yes, Dad."

Doctor John interrupted, shifting the conversation. "Eva's mother?"

"Yes?"

"Before I release your daughter, I need proof that you are her real parents."

Eva's mother hesitated. "Yes, please, go on."

Doctor John's voice turned sharper. "Out of the things , you have done. Confess your greatest sin."

"What?" Eva's mother gasped.

"Tell me the most shameful thing you've ever done… then I return your daughter to you," he insisted.

Eva erupted in fury, lunging at Doctor John despite her cuffs. "You're a monster! A devil! I'll kill you!" she screamed.

With brutal efficiency, Doctor John slammed her head onto the desk, pinning her down. His voice was soft, mocking. "See how far your mother will go to save you."

Eva's mother was now trapped, torn between her daughter and the demand. "What sin?" she asked, her voice shaking.

"Think carefully. I'm sure you already have something in mind."

Her husband interjected, "This is too much!"

Detective Reynolds cautioned, "Sir, don't provoke him."

"But this is too cruel! In front of all these people, in front of her daughter?"

Detective Reynolds whispered urgently, "It doesn't have to be true. Just say something. No one will know if it's real."

Doctor John spoke again, his tone growing colder. "If you don't confess…"

Eva's mother blurted out, "I bribed my way into a contract. I didn't think it was wrong—everyone does it! I also hired a detective to dig up dirt on an employee so I could fire him. He was in the union, so I spread rumors that he was a gambler, an alcoholic. I forced him to resign."

Doctor John sighed. "Ma'am. Ma'am. I don't want to hear your trivial sins. I need a confession that proves you are her mother. The first sin that came to mind when I asked."

Eva, realizing what was coming, began to cry.

Her mother's voice cracked. "Just tell me what it is."

"You already know," Doctor John said simply.

Meanwhile, Michael navigated the dark hallways, carefully avoiding windows. His mind raced, searching for a way to help.

In the teachers' dorm, Jason whispered, "He's trying to ruin us. Completely destroy us."

Back in the broadcasting room, Doctor John turned to Eva. "What do you think? Will your mother confess? Will she choose you... or herself?"

Doctor John spoke to Eva's mom again. "You leave me no choice. I will count to ten. If you want your daughter back alive, you know what to do." His voice was cold and calculating as he counted down the seconds.

The countdown began. "Ten... nine... eight..."

The room fell into unbearable silence. Eva's mother, tearful, remained silent.

At zero, Doctor John sighed and looked down at Eva, her tears a testament to the painful reality of her situation—her mother had chosen herself.

As Doctor John began to lead Eva out of the room, he finally voiced his thoughts aloud.

"I guess mothers don't risk their lives for their daughters after all. I had hoped she would, but your mother... she's just selfish. She chose herself over you. You shouldn't be upset, though. You won't try to slit your wrists again because of her, will you?"

His words stung. Eva glared at him, her voice filled with fury. "I hope you die."

Doctor John patted her on the head like a child. "Don't worry, Eva. You'll be fine."

Eva was released. Her mother rushed to embrace her, but Eva's face remained cold and distant.

Detective Reynolds immediately pulled Eva aside for information. "How many bullets does he have left?"

Eva hesitated, then answered. "Three, at most."

Meanwhile, Michael retrieved his laptop in the cafeteria, scanning CCTV footage for anything useful.

Back in the teachers' dorm, Jason, Richard, and David sat listening to the announcements. As soon as they heard that Jason's parents and Richard's father had arrived, Jason sprang to his feet.

Jason rushed to the door—already locked—and added a bicycle lock for good measure.

"We're safe now," he said, snapping the lock into place. "Doctor John can't open this door. We should've done this earlier."

Doctor John arrived at the same moment, unimpressed by the lock. "So that's your choice?" he mused. "That's fine too. You can stay locked in there… just remember, Frank will die in your place. I've hidden him somewhere in the school."

Jason sneered. "Shut up. Why do you care what I do?"

Doctor John's smirk didn't fade. "You're right, no one can criticize you. Frank himself said he was the most sinful among you. This is a fitting way to end it."

His words were a knife in the gut.

Doctor John turned to Richard. "And you, Richard… You're used to living like this, aren't you?"

That was the last straw. Richard, trembling, unlocked the door. Doctor John smiled. He had won.

Michael, working quietly in the broadcasting room, had rigged the CCTV feed to project onto the school's jumbotron. The police outside could see everything—including Amanda's lifeless body.

Eva gasped. "There's a hidden passage!" She pointed to a window where David had outlined an escape route. SWAT teams immediately began crawling through the air ducts.

In the broadcasting room, Michael hid under a desk as Doctor John addressed Richard's father.

"Sir, you have a wonderful son. I was confused at first, but among these students, he is the true leader. But as a psychologist, I see his heroism as a death wish. He must feel guilty for surviving instead of his mother, as if he has to grow up to be great in her place. Did you raise him that way? Sir, I really like Richard. Please," Doctor John urged, "tell him not to be attached to death. Tell him not to think about dying for someone else."

Richard's father, pleaded, "Richard… Please… Don't die. That's all I ask. No matter what, don't die. Even if it means being a coward—just live."

Before anything could settle, Jason's mother screamed, "Where's my son?! I see all the other children, but not Jason!"

Panic erupted outside. Officers hurriedly escorted her away.

Doctor John whispered to himself, "They're watching me."

Inside, SWAT teams moved in, rescuing Frank and Jason and David while parents and police watched anxiously.

Doctor John led Richard to the rooftop.

Later, a gunshot rang out.

Eva screamed, fearing Richard was dead.

But on the rooftop, Richard lay motionless—alive.

***

Richard lay unconscious in a hospital bed, while his father sat nearby, watching the news.

The TV anchor reported, "Despite being reported to the police, students were held hostage for eight days. The police are under scrutiny for their delayed response. All school officials have refused to comment. The criminal, a psychologist from an elite medical university, took his own life at the end of the case. The students are now receiving treatment."

As the news played, Richard stirred, his eyelids fluttering open. "Dad," he murmured.

His father quickly switched off the TV and turned to him.

Richard struggled to sit up. "Where are the others?"

Richard made his way to Steve's hospital room, where Michael and David were drawing on Steve's cast, while Frank and Jason stood nearby.

David grinned when he saw him. "Mr. Fainter finally woke up!"

Michael, Frank, and David immediately checked Richard's head.

Richard winced. "It hurts. I think my brain is damaged."

Steve smirked and reached out to touch David's head in return. Richard frowned. "What's wrong with you?"

Steve chuckled. "I just wanted to see what a bump feels like."

Laughter filled the room, momentarily easing the weight of their shared trauma.

Detective Reynolds entered the room, accompanied by his colleague. "It's great to see you all alive," he said. "There are a few things I need to confirm. But first, I have some good news—your teacher is alive and being treated in this hospital."

Everyone froze.

"That's impossible!" they exclaimed in unison.

"Liam was dead for days in the courtyard!" Richard said in disbelief.

Michael added, "He was in the center for several days!"

"Center?" Detective Reynolds asked.

Richard clarified, "The garden in the middle of the school."

Detective Reynolds took a deep breath. "That's where we found the body of Doctor John. He appeared to have shot himself and fallen from the roof—after he hit you, Richard."

Richard's blood ran cold.

"But Liam... Liam was found on the roof," Reynolds continued. "We had mistaken Liam's body for Doctor John's."

***

Meanwhile, in a lavish home, Gary was recovering in his room. After the doctors and nurses left, he was alone with his mother.

"Mom," he said quietly. "Why did my caretaker kidnap me? She was always so nice... I even mistook her for you."

His mother's face remained cold. "Because I fired her," she answered.

"Why?"

His mother's voice was sharp. "Because you thought she was your mother. You gave her a Mother's Day carnation instead of me. You thought mothers don't get hurt by their children."

She turned and left, leaving him alone.

As Gary wandered the house, avoiding the Monster in the Corner, a call came. The maid brought him the phone.

"It's Richard," she said.

But when Gary put the phone to his ear, it wasn't Richard's voice. It was Doctor John's. Counting to ten. The Monster in the Corner began counting too.

Memories flooded back—of when he was kidnapped as a child.

He remembered his caretaker's son cooking pancakes for him. "I'm hungry," Gary had said, hugging her.

"Just wait one minute, almost finished," she had replied.

"No," Gary had insisted.

"Okay! Let's play hide and seek," she said. "You go hide. I'll count to ten and find you."

Gary had searched for a hiding place and finally opened the cupboard—only to find a dead boy inside, his face half-blue.

The caretaker had stormed in, grabbing him as he sobbed.

"Stop crying!" she had yelled. "This is your fault! You killed my son! While I was busy taking care of you, my child—my poor baby—got sick. He developed cyanosis. We had just started his treatment. We thought your rich mother would help us, that your family would step in. But what did we get in return? They fired me!"

Her voice cracked.

"We couldn't afford the treatment... and my baby died, because of you, because of your family."

Then she had painted his face blue and whispered, "Now you'll live as my son."

The police stormed in. The caretaker held a knife to Gary, taking him hostage, but the officers reacted quickly and shot her to save him.

Blood pooled beside her and the blue-faced boy.

Now, upstairs in his present-day home, Gary shut his door.

Outside, armed guards flinched at the sound of a gunshot.

***

Back at the hospital, Michael peered out the window at the police checkpoints. "They're everywhere," he noted.

David sighed. "Doctor John is really good. He outplayed the police—even us."

Frank hesitated. "Do you think he's trying to escape?"

Richard shook his head. "He had plenty of chances to escape."

But Steve disagreed. "If I were him, there's only one thing I'd want—to confirm the results of my experiment."

***

Meanwhile, at Gary's house, police stormed in. They found Gary's lifeless body on the floor, a hunting rifle beside him. Blood seeped from his head.

Half of his face was painted blue.

***

At the Steve's hospital room, Detective Reynolds entered the room. David asked, "Did you catch Doctor John?"

Detective Reynolds exhaled deeply. "Not yet..." He paused before continuing, "A little while ago, Gary... took his own life," he said quietly.

The news hit them like a punch to the gut. Gary—their friend, their companion—was gone. Everyone in the room looked saddened, and Eva cried.

Detective Reynolds continued speaking with Richard, Michael, Eva, Frank, Jason, David, and Steve.

He revealed that Gary had shot himself with his father's gun. One side of his face was blue, and he had left a suicide note mentioning, "the eggs about to crack." "Do you know what this means?" Detective Reynolds inquired.

Jason responded, "The monster egg!"

Detective Reynolds nodded and added, "He received a phone call at his home number; the caller claimed to be Richard."

Frank interjected, "But Richard was here with us the whole time!"

Detective Reynolds concluded, "From now on, all contact with the outside will be cut off." He then left the room.

Richard, troubled, murmured, "I'm sure it was Doctor John who spoke to Gary. What did he say to him to make him kill himself?"

Steve glanced at Richard, and together, they stepped outside to discuss further.

Later, at the police station, an officer received a call.

"This is Doctor John," the voice said. "I want to say goodbye. I have finished my final experiment. Please tell the students goodbye for me."

The officer's hands shook. But the voice wasn't Doctor John's. It was Steve's. The officers, unable to discern the difference, assumed it was the doctor himself.

After the call, Richard and Steve threw the cell phone out of the window, aiming for the garbage truck below. Soon after, a garbage truck departed from the hospital, prompting the police to scramble away from their posts.

Unbeknownst to them, Doctor John was already in the hospital, disguised as a doctor.

Later, Detective Reynolds and other officers pursued the garbage truck where Richard had discarded his cell phone. They traced the bus and continued their chase.

Meanwhile, David held back the two remaining guards, allowing Richard, Jason, Steve, Frank, Michael, and the others to slip away undetected. One guard remarked to David, "You're interrupting public duty." David retorted, "The criminal is outside; we don't have to stay here!"

Elsewhere in the hospital, Eva's mother shadowed her every move, concern etched on her face. As Eva was leaving, her mother asked, "Where are you going?"

Eva replied, "I'm going to the convenience store!" Her mother insisted, "Let's go together!" Eva refused, "No." Her mother pressed, "I have to buy something too."

Eva snapped, her words sharp, "I said no, what's wrong with you?" Her mother, taken aback, responded, "Don't you know how I feel, what if he captures you again!"

Eva had had enough. She retorted bitterly, "If I were so precious, why didn't you answer?" Her mother, caught off guard, flushed red, struggling to defend herself. She stammered, "What do you mean?"

Eva coldly threw her mother's past affair back in her face, "Your greatest sin." Her mother stood wide-eyed, unable to respond as Eva stormed off.

***

Meanwhile, Detective Reynolds and his team successfully intercepted the garbage truck on the road a short distance from the hospital. They recovered Richard's cell phone but found no trace of Doctor John.

***

Eva walked toward the hospital roof, stopping at the edge.

Doctor John approached. "Don't act that way toward your mother," he mused. "If only emotions were simple. Just hate, just love, just fear. Life would be much easier."

Eva's eyes were unwavering. "You lost."

Doctor John smirked—until he saw Jason, Richard, Michael, Steve, David, and Frank behind him. It had been a trap all along.

"You're all here," Doctor John remarked.

Michael replied, "Except one... Gary is missing."

Richard's fists clenched. "Did you call Gary?"

Doctor John nodded.

"What did you say?"

"I simply said hello," he replied. "And whispered the final keyword to awaken the monster."

Eva stepped forward. "You lost. The monster didn't wake up."

Doctor John's smile faded. "How can you be sure?"

"Gary is dead," Eva stated coldly. "Want me to say it again? Gary took his own life. He didn't become a monster. You wanted us to become monsters, you wanted to prove that you weren't the only monster. but you were wrong. You're the only monster here."

Jason stepped forward. "It's over."

Doctor John smirked. "One failure doesn't invalidate a hypothesis. My experiment isn't over yet. I admit that Gary was a failed case, but what about the rest of you?"

"You failed," Richard said.

Detective Reynolds and the other officers rushed back to the hospital, heading toward the roof. As they heard the police sirens, Steve asked, "Did you plan to get caught from the beginning?"

Doctor John replied, "I don't know; anyway, I surrender."

Richard moved toward the entrance door and locked it.

Richard, joined by Jason, David, Frank, and Michael, seized Doctor John, pushing him toward the edge of the roof. Standing tall, Richard declared, "It's over."

Doctor John looked into Richard's eyes one last time. And then, they let go. Doctor John body plummeted to the ground, mere seconds before the police breached the rooftop door.

Before Doctor John hit the ground, he smiled.

***

In the police interrogation room, Frank sat alone. Detective Reynolds stood before him, pressing for answers.

"Have you rested well?" the detective asked.

"Yes," Frank replied.

"Did you sleep well?"

"Yes."

Reynolds nodded slowly. "Tell me one more time—what happened on the roof?"

Frank took a breath and began.

"I was getting coffee from the vending machine when I saw someone who looked like Doctor John heading to the roof. I went to Steve's room to tell everyone."

In another interrogation room, Detective Reynolds asked Eva the same question.

"I had a fight with my mom and went up to the roof. Doctor John came from behind," Eva said.

Elsewhere, Michael, Jason, David, and Steve were also being questioned.

"After Frank told us he saw Doctor John going to the roof, we all went up," Michael said.

"Doctor John was already holding Eva hostage," Steve added. "He was holding her neck, standing at the edge of the roof."

"Then Doctor John ordered me to close the door," Jason said.

"And after Jason locked it, we heard police sirens," Steve continued. "Doctor John looked away for a second. Richard ran to save Eva. He didn't mean to, but when he reached him, he pushed Doctor John. Then Doctor John lost his balance and fell."

It was a story they had rehearsed. Practiced together. Memorized to keep every detail consistent.

One by one, they gave their versions—meticulously crafted, perfectly aligned with the truth they had chosen.

Finally, Detective Reynolds turned to Richard.

Richard sat quietly, his eyes vacant, his voice flat as he continued the story.

"Doctor John just... fell off the roof. The police came afterward."

Detective Reynolds asked. "You didn't have time to do anything?"

"That's right."

The detective stared at him for a moment longer, but there was nothing to challenge. The statements matched. No contradictions.

Detective Reynolds nodded. "Did Doctor John say anything before he died?"

Richard didn't blink. "No. He didn't say a thing."

And just like that, Richard was free.

Outside the interrogation room, the others—Jason, Steve, Michael, Frank, David, and Eva—waited for him. As he stepped into the hallway, they fell into quiet step beside him.

They walked together in silence.

But in Richard's mind, the words echoed—chilling and unforgettable.

"I won."

Manufactured by Amazon.ca
Acheson, AB